THE RIVALRY

ALSO BY JOHN FEINSTEIN

John Feinstein

THE RIVALRY

MYSTERY
AT
THE ARMY-NAVY GAME

ALFRED A. KNOPF

New York

THIS IS A BORZOI BOOK PUBLISHED BY ALFRED A. KNOPF

Visit us on the Web! www.randomhouse.com/kids

Educators and librarians, for a variety of teaching tools, visit us at
www.randomhouse.com/teachers

Library of Congress Cataloging-in-Publication Data
Feinstein, John.
The rivalry : mystery at the Army-Navy game / John Feinstein. — 1st ed.
p. cm.
Summary: Eighth-grade sportswriters Stevie and Susan Carol team up to solve a mystery at the famous Army-Navy football game.
ISBN 978-0-375-86570-1 (trade) — ISBN 978-0-375-96570-8 (lib. bdg.) —
ISBN 978-0-375-89603-3 (ebook) — ISBN 978-0-375-85816-1 (pbk.)
1. Journalism—Fiction. 2. Army-Navy Football Game—Fiction. 3. Football—Fiction.
4. Mystery and detective stories.] I. Title.
PZ7.F3343Ri 2010
[Fic]—dc22
2010019614

The text of this book is set in 12-point Goudy.

Printed in the United States of America
September 2010
10 9 8 7 6 5 4 3 2 1

First Edition

*This book is for Jim Cantelupe, Joel Davis,
Garrett Smith, and Andrew Thompson—my Army-Navy
captains—and for all their teammates,
past, present, and future. . . .*

GAME DAY: 3 HOURS TO KICKOFF

"**H**ere they come."

At the sound of Susan Carol Anderson's voice, Stevie Thomas instantly did two things: he turned to look at the tunnel at the far end of FedEx Field, where the Naval Academy band would be emerging at any moment, and he also stood up very straight because that was always what he did when standing next to Susan Carol.

From underneath the stadium he could now hear "Anchors Aweigh," the Navy fight song. He had memorized the words to both "Anchors Aweigh" and "On, Brave Old Army Team" in the past two weeks.

Sure enough, the band was marching out of the tunnel. It was three hours before kickoff of the Army-Navy game, but the stands on both sides of the stadium were more than half full.

The game was scheduled to start at precisely 12:08 p.m., and Stevie and Susan Carol had arrived at the stadium with Bobby Kelleher and Tamara Mearns shortly after 7:00 a.m. Kelleher and Mearns were married and both columnists, but they worked for rival papers—Kelleher for the *Washington Herald*, Mearns for the *Washington Post*. They had become unofficial mentors to the two aspiring teenage journalists, but Stevie and Susan Carol had covered so many major sporting events in the past couple years that they felt like old pros. And so the four of them chatted comfortably on the sidelines as the traditional march-ons began.

First the entire student body of Annapolis would march onto the field, followed by the entire student body of West Point. Stevie now knew a good deal about both Army and Navy, having spent much of the last few weeks at the two academies.

"Ladies and gentlemen," the PA announcer said, "please welcome, from the United States Naval Academy, the Brigade of Midshipmen!"

The band peeled to the left to start working its way up the far sideline, and Stevie could see the first of Navy's thirty-two companies marching into the stadium. To Stevie it looked as if the mids were marching in lockstep, about ten across as they followed their company commander onto the field.

But Kelleher was shaking his head. "They can't march," he said, a smile on his face. "Look at them, they're practically loping."

"Who needs to march on a boat?" Mearns asked.

"Yeah, yeah," Kelleher said. "But they almost never practice except the week of this game. The Army kids march all the time."

"Spoken like an Army fan, Bobby," Susan Carol said, her lilting North Carolina accent in full force. "You showin' bias already?"

Everyone laughed as the third company arrived on the field. "Look, I've told you, Susan Carol, I grew up in New York, but I've been around Navy ever since I came to Washington. I have no biases."

"Don't you always say that everyone has biases and we just have to be aware of them?" Stevie said.

Kelleher looked at him and shook his head. "That's the problem with fourteen-year-olds," he said. "They're always listening when you talk."

"Don't believe it, Bobby," Susan Carol said.

As each new group began its march into the stadium, the announcer would say the company's name and the names of their company leaders, and cheers would rise up from the crowd.

Two men strode purposefully toward them down the sidelines. Pete Dowling was tall, with close-cropped graying hair, and Bob Campbell had jet-black hair, but otherwise they were hard to tell apart in their Secret Service uniforms: dark suit, sunglasses, and wires running from their shirt collars up to their right ears.

"How's it looking?" Kelleher asked Dowling as the two men approached.

"Worst problem we've had is some fans trying to smuggle in alcohol," Dowling said. "Cold as it is, I don't really blame them."

It was a chilly morning—only about thirty-five degrees. But the sky was clear, and with the sun shining, it would warm up by game time. Football in December—it was bound to be cold.

Campbell turned to Stevie and Susan Carol. "Quite a sight, isn't it?"

"Yes! And it's a fabulous view from here." Susan Carol had accompanied Campbell on a security sweep earlier, and the two hours had been mind-numbingly dull—which was okay with her. She'd had enough excitement in the past week. They had gone from one luxury box to another while Campbell made certain that every nook and cranny had been checked and rechecked by agents and police and bomb-sniffing dogs.

Their tour had concluded in the incredibly plush owner's box, which was where the president would sit during the first half of the game. Then he would cross the field at halftime, as was tradition, and sit in a specially constructed box on the Navy side during the second half.

Susan Carol couldn't help but notice that, other than the luxury-box area, the stadium was kind of a dump—even with all the bunting that had been hung for the game. A lot of the seats were at bad angles; there were some with almost no view of the field at all. It was a good reminder of how lucky she was to be here on the sidelines.

"Bobby's been pointing out that the Navy guys can't march," Stevie said.

"Bobby's an Army fan," Agent Dowling said. "But he's right anyway."

"Look, I always say Army wins the march-on and Navy wins the playing of the alma maters when the game's over," Kelleher said. "'Blue and Gold' is a much better song than 'Alma Mater.'"

Mearns looked carefully at Dowling. "You're serious? There's nothing going on that makes you nervous? We're still not quoting you on anything."

Dowling nodded. "You guys have been as good as your word on that. If something *was* going on, I'd at least say I couldn't tell you. But it's all quiet so far. Everything has been checked and we'll do another sweep of all the locker rooms, the tunnels, and the field before the president gets here."

"Still on schedule for eleven forty?" Kelleher asked.

"Wheels down on his helicopter outside at eleven thirty-five," Campbell said, glancing at his watch. "He'll meet the teams, flip the coin, and we'll get him up to his box in time for kickoff."

Stevie was still a little bit nervous. The past two weeks had been eventful, to say the least. Plus, his history at major sporting events with Susan Carol made it almost certain that *something* was going to happen before the day was over.

The Brigade of Midshipmen, all four thousand of them,

were now spread out across the entire field in thirty-two perfect units. They were staring straight ahead, facing the Navy fans. It was an impressive sight, and the fans thought so too—they were all on their feet cheering.

Suddenly, all four thousand midshipmen pivoted—as one—to turn and face the Army fans.

"A-R-M-Y—goooooo, ARMY!" they said together, doffing their caps as they finished. Applause and a few cheers came from the Army fans, most of them dressed in black and gold.

The midshipmen stood still for a few seconds, caps still in the air. Then, again as one, they put them smartly back on their heads, paused, and pivoted so they were facing the Navy fans again.

"N-A-V-Y—GOOOOOOOOOOO, NAVY!!!!" Their combined voices were about five times as loud.

Stevie felt a chill as the Navy fans erupted, and for once it wasn't the cold. He had really come to appreciate all the Army and Navy traditions in the past two weeks, and this pageantry was like nothing he had ever experienced before.

The midshipmen started to make their way off the field toward the far corner of the stands where they would be seated—although they wouldn't sit at any point throughout the afternoon, once the game began.

And Stevie was anxious for the game to begin. He'd almost lost sight of the game itself amid all the threats and intrigue that had been swirling around. It'd make a great story once it was all over, he felt sure. But a lot still had to happen in the next few hours.

As Dowling reminded him, saying, "Come on, Steve, we've got the first important assignment of the day."

"What's that?" Stevie asked.

"We have to deliver a gun," Dowling said.

FRIDAY NIGHT
AT THE PALESTRA

The Army-Navy misadventure began innocently enough, a chance for Stevie to do the two things he enjoyed most in life: being a sportswriter covering a big event and hanging out with Susan Carol.

Stevie was doing one of those two things on a wintry Friday night about a month earlier. He was sitting on press row at the Palestra, no more than a three-point-shot attempt away from the St. Joseph's bench.

There was a time-out with just twenty-five seconds left in the game, and Villanova led St. Joe's 67–65. The din of nearly ten thousand fans packed into the ancient gym was so loud it was difficult to hear anything.

"If St. Joe's pulls this out, Jay will never hear the end of it," Dick Jerardi, sitting to Stevie's left, was saying, leaning close so Stevie could hear him. "They could go on and win the Big East, and all the Villanova fans are going to say is, 'But you lost to St. Joe's.'"

Stevie laughed. He knew the longtime *Philadelphia Daily News* reporter was right. As successful as Jay Wright had been during his coaching tenure at Villanova—including a run to the Final Four in 2009—his school's fans found any loss to another Big Five school—St. Joseph's, La Salle, Temple, or Pennsylvania—completely unacceptable.

Stevie noticed the St. Joseph's Hawk mascot standing on the edge of the huddle, flapping his wings as always. St. Joseph's motto was "The Hawk will never die," and the student wearing the costume was required to keep his arms flapping at all times throughout a game. Given the difficulty of that task, Stevie hadn't been surprised to learn that whoever was selected as the mascot received a full scholarship for that year.

Even though he really liked Jay Wright and Villanova, Stevie was rooting for St. Joseph's to pull off an upset. For one thing, a win would mean more to the Hawks, who were unranked starting the new season. And he liked Phil Martelli's everyman approach to coaching. Wright was just so smooth—known as one of the best-dressed coaches in the country. Jerardi had told him that Wright wore cologne *during* games.

TV finally came back from commercial and St. Joe's inbounded. The ball swung to point guard Tommy Jones and he slowly dribbled the clock down. "Oh God," Jerardi murmured. "They're going for the win right now."

The clock ticked under ten seconds. Jones began to approach the key. Out of the corner of his eye, Stevie saw St. Joe's best shooter, Michael Anthony, cutting from the left baseline to the right, getting a screen to prevent his defender from following. Stevie knew what was coming next.

Sure enough, as Jones spun into the lane, Anthony popped out on the right side of the key. Jones got him the ball as the Villanova defenders scrambled. Stevie could see the clock . . . three . . . two . . .

Anthony caught the ball with the clock at two seconds and took one quick dribble to square himself and clear some space. He was just outside the three-point line when he released the shot, and the buzzer sounded with the ball in the air.

Swish.

The St. Joseph's fans exploded! Anthony disappeared under a pile of teammates. The coaches met right in front of where Stevie was sitting to shake hands.

"Gutsy call," Wright said, an arm around Martelli's shoulders.

"I got lucky," Martelli shouted back.

Stevie double-checked the scoreboard: St. Joseph's 68–Villanova 67.

Martelli was right. He was lucky. He would have been second-guessed for days—maybe years in Philly—if the do-or-die shot hadn't fallen.

But Stevie was luckier still. It was an amazing game, and he got to write about it and tell the tale.

* * *

Stevie was also lucky that the Villanova–St. Joseph's game was played on a Friday night. He wasn't allowed to cover games on school nights, his parents being a lot more concerned with how he was doing as a high school freshman than his budding career as a sportswriter.

Stevie had almost fallen into it, winning a writing contest when he was thirteen that allowed him to go to the Final Four. There he and Susan Carol, the other contest winner, had stumbled into a plot to fix the national championship game. Thanks to the fact that they had broken that story, the two of them had been asked to cover other events.

Now Stevie wrote for the *Washington Herald* whenever he could, and Susan Carol wrote for the *Washington Post*. And he'd found a girlfriend as well as a job. Even though they had endured some seriously rocky moments, Stevie and Susan Carol were going out—well, as much as you could when one person lived in Philadelphia and the other lived in Goldsboro, North Carolina.

As Stevie made his way through the celebrating St. Joseph's fans to the interview room that was underneath the stands, he noticed he had a text message on his phone from Bobby Kelleher: *Call as soon as u can. Great game.*

Stevie figured it would be at least ten minutes before any players or coaches came in to talk to the media, so he found a corner where his phone got service and dialed Kelleher's number.

"Man, Phil took a hell of a chance playing for one shot," Kelleher said, answering the call.

"Where are you?" Stevie asked, because it sounded almost as loud on Kelleher's end as on his.

"I'm in a sports bar down the street from the Penn State campus," Kelleher said. "I watched the game with Hoops. It absolutely killed him not being there."

Stevie smiled. Hoops was Dick Weiss, a columnist for the *New York Daily News*. Weiss was a born-and-bred Philadelphian who had grown up watching games in the Palestra. Even though he worked for a New York paper, he still lived in Philadelphia and would always be a Philly guy at heart.

But Kelleher and Weiss were both covering the Penn State–Ohio State football game the next day, which had a noon kickoff, so they had to settle for watching the basketball game on TV.

"Hey, Hoops wants to say hi," Kelleher said.

A moment later, Weiss was on the phone. Even over the noise, his Philadelphia accent was distinctive. "You have to ask Phil what he was doing on the last play, okai?" he said. "He was vurry, vurry lucky that shot went down."

Stevie agreed, and they made plans to see a game in December when the regular football season was over and Weiss had some free time. Then Kelleher came back on the line.

"Anyway, you think you can take the train down to Washington on Sunday?" he said. "You can tell your folks you'll be there and back in a few hours." Reading Stevie's mind, he added, "You can do your homework on the train."

"I'll ask," Stevie said. "What do you need, a Redskins sidebar or something?"

"Hardly. I wouldn't do that to you. No, we're having a big planning meeting over at the *Post*. Army-Navy will be in DC in a couple weeks and the two papers are combining coverage and going all out. First time the game's ever been played in DC, and it may be the last. Both papers want you and Susan Carol involved."

"Is Susan Carol going to be there Sunday?" Stevie asked.

He heard Kelleher laugh. "Yes, Stevie, I figured that'd get you here. Typical her: she's managed to get an interview with Orrin Hatch on Monday to talk about his legislation to ban the BCS. She's going to stay with us Sunday night."

Stevie shook his head. That *was* typical Susan Carol. She was always one step ahead.

"When did you call her?" Stevie wondered.

"This afternoon. Don't ask me how she got the interview set up so fast, because I haven't a clue. Talk to your parents. You've probably got a short school week coming up with Thanksgiving, and you won't miss more than a day or two of school to cover the game. You've pulled it off in the past."

Barely, Stevie thought. Still, especially with Susan Carol involved, the Army-Navy game sounded like fun.

He heard someone call his name and saw Dick Jerardi waving him in the direction of the interview room.

"Martelli's coming in," he said. "Gotta go."

"Call me in the morning," Kelleher said. "I'll be up early fighting traffic to get to the stadium." Stevie rolled his eyes. After sports, Bobby's biggest obsessions were traffic and parking.

Stevie hustled into the interview room just as Martelli was talking about the last shot.

"I think I probably lost my mind during the time-out with twenty-five seconds left," he said. "I know, it's crazy playing for one shot there. But something in my gut just told me this was the way to go. Fortunately, Anthony made me look like a good coach by making the shot."

Stevie scribbled furiously in his notebook. That took care of Weiss's question. Now all he had to do was convince his parents to let him take the train to Washington on Sunday.

A POST ASSIGNMENT

Stevie waited until breakfast the next morning to bring up the Washington trip to his parents. He knew his mother would need convincing, and he had been too tired when he got home from the game to start a debate.

"How much homework do you have this weekend?" his mom asked, a predictable and reasonable first question.

"Not much," Stevie lied.

His father looked at him sharply. "I thought you told me you had a paper due on *Beowulf*, but you'd pass on watching the football games today to get it done," he said.

"Well, I can still do that," Stevie answered. "And I can do the rest on the train."

His parents looked at one another. Christine Thomas shrugged helplessly. "I know you're going to let him do it, Bill," she said. "You always do."

"It's not as if he's flunking out of school," Bill Thomas said. "He's making solid B's."

"Which these days might get him into a solid B-grade college—but not anyplace that's any good," she said.

"Mom, not everyone needs to go to an Ivy League school," Stevie said. His dad had gone to Penn and his mother to Columbia. They had met in law school at Yale.

"All he's done with journalism will help him a lot, Chris," Bill Thomas said. "Plus, can we worry about college when he's, I don't know, a junior?"

"Okay, okay, I know when I'm outnumbered," she said. "Stevie, I want to *see* the *Beowulf* paper before you get on that train."

"You got it, Mom." He raced off to call Kelleher before she could change her mind.

By ten the next morning, he was on a train out of 30th Street station. He had only written half the *Beowulf* paper, but the fact that it was actually pretty good rescued him. "Come home with the paper unfinished and you won't get to work on this project," his mother had said.

He quickly read the sports section of the *New York Times*—having read the *Philadelphia Inquirer* at home— and then dug into his math and Spanish homework. The trip to Union Station in Washington took a little under two hours, and he was just about finished when it arrived. That left *Beowulf* to finish on the ride home.

He had been in Union Station before, so he knew exactly how to work his way from the tracks through the massive building to the front door that led to the cab line. It was a cold but sunny November day, and he could see the enormous white dome of the Capitol building shining in the distance—impressive.

He got a cab to the *Washington Post* offices, as Kelleher had instructed. When Stevie had called the day before to say he could come, Bobby had explained the details of the project to him.

"We started combining some coverage with the *Post* about a year ago," he said. "The point is to save money, really. Instead of both papers sending people to cover a mid-May road game for the Nationals in Chicago, one reporter goes and files for both papers. If someone writes a day story on how Maryland is getting ready to play Wake Forest in football, both papers may use it.

"This is different, though. We both want to do blow-out coverage of Army-Navy because it's never been in DC before and because both teams are good this year. We got lucky with that. But we don't have as much staff as we used to before the economy slammed us and both papers had buyouts. A lot of talent walked out the doors. So the editors decided we'd work together. Which means we can team you and Susan Carol."

Stevie certainly liked that idea. She was the prettiest girl he'd ever met, scary smart, and she knew more about sports than he did—which could actually be a little annoying, if Stevie was honest.

Still, she kept him on his toes, and there was nothing more fun than hanging out with her at a major event—even if they did seem to get into trouble most of the time.

His father had once likened them to Pigpen, a character in the old "Peanuts" comic strip who went around in a swirl of dust and dirt. "That's you and Susan Carol when it comes to trouble," he had said. "It just follows you wherever you go."

The cab ride only took about ten minutes, and when he arrived at the *Post*, Stevie called Matt Rennie. Rennie had been Kelleher's editor at the *Washington Herald* but had moved to the *Post* when he had been offered the number-two job on the *Post*'s sports staff.

"Steve, glad you could make it," Rennie said. "I'll meet you in the lobby."

Rennie walked him through security and then brought him up to the newsroom on the fifth floor.

"You're the first one here," Rennie said. "Bobby, Tamara, and Susan Carol are on their way in from Potomac. If you want, I'll give you a quick tour."

Stevie loved that idea. He had recently read *All the President's Men*, the book written by *Post* reporters Bob Woodward and Carl Bernstein about the fall of President Richard Nixon, much of it stemming from reporting they had done after the infamous 1972 break-in at the Watergate Hotel office building. He had been fascinated by the story of how Woodward and Bernstein slowly pieced the story together, beginning on the day after the break-in, when it had appeared to be little more than a routine burglary attempt.

He knew the newspaper business had changed a lot since then, but just being in the *Post* newsroom gave him a thrill. It was massive—and oddly quiet.

"Not a lot of people in this early," Rennie said. "The dot-com people are here, and a few editors and reporters, but Sundays are normally like this. I think Woodward's in, though. Bobby told me you wanted to meet him."

"Bob Woodward's here?"

"He was on *Meet the Press* this morning. He sometimes swings by for a little while on Sundays just because it's so quiet."

They were walking between desks toward the back of the newsroom and Stevie was getting a little nervous. He'd met a lot of famous athletes and coaches, but Bob Woodward was the epitome of what Stevie hoped to someday be. He knew he'd never be an NFL quarterback or an NBA point guard. A top-flight journalist? Maybe.

"Hey, Bob, you busy?" Rennie said, poking his head into an open doorway.

"Not at all, Matt, come in," Stevie heard a voice say from inside the door.

"Got someone here I'd like to introduce you to," Rennie said. "Bob Woodward, this is Steve Thomas."

Woodward stood up and walked around his desk, hand extended. He was medium height, with dark hair, graying at the temples. Stevie knew he was in his sixties, but he looked younger.

"Hi, Steve, I'm Bob Woodward," he said. "Very nice to have you here at the *Post*."

He had a friendly smile and spoke slowly in one of those flat midwestern accents. *Have* came out "heav."

"Bobby called this morning and said you might come by," Woodward continued as they shook hands. "Why don't you have a seat? I hear you've had quite a reporting career already." *Reporting* came out "reporting," but what was funny was Woodward talking about *Stevie's* reporting career. He was tempted to say something like "Yeah, I hear your career hasn't been half bad either."

"Well, we've gotten lucky a few times," he said. "Susan Carol and I, that is. She's sort of been my partner."

Woodward was nodding. "I know," he said. "I've read some of the stories you two have done together. Luck will carry you only so far. You two have done a lot of excellent reporting."

"I just finished reading *All the President's Men*, and I think it's fair to say that you and Carl Bernstein did some reporting"—he almost said "reporting" but caught himself—"that was pretty excellent."

Woodward laughed. "Now, we *did* get lucky," he said. "We were lucky that Nixon and his men weren't terribly smart."

"Well, it was a great book."

Rennie chimed in, "And then you were lucky to have Robert Redford play you in the movie version."

"No, *that* was embarrassing," Woodward said. "The funny thing is, Dustin Hoffman actually looked a lot like Carl. Needless to say, I don't look anything like Bob."

"Bob?" Stevie said.

"Oh, sorry, yeah, Redford. He goes by Bob. We actually became pretty good friends. Hey, did Bobby ever tell you about the time I introduced them?"

They were both shaking their heads now. "Bob came to see me in the newsroom one day. Bobby was walking past my office, so I waved him in and said, 'Bobby Kelleher, meet Bob Redford.' Bobby shook hands with him and said, 'So, Bob, where do you work?'"

"He didn't recognize Robert Redford?" Rennie asked, clearly amazed.

Woodward nodded. "Now, Bob is shorter in person than he seems on-screen and he was wearing glasses. But still . . ."

"So what happened?" Stevie asked.

"I said, 'Bobby, Bob starred in your all-time favorite movie, the one you told me you saw three times in the same day.' It took a minute, but then it dawned on him. All he could do was babble about how sorry he was after that. You don't often see Bobby Kelleher completely flustered, but he was that time."

Rennie stood up. His cell phone had just gone off. "Everyone's here," he announced to Stevie. "Bob, I want to thank you for making my day and maybe my month with that story."

"Be sure to ask him about it," Woodward said. "I'm

certain he'd love to be reminded. Steve, it was a pleasure to meet you. I can't wait to read what you come up with on this Army-Navy project."

"What are you working on these days?" Stevie asked, caught up in the one-reporter-to-another repartee.

"A book on President Obama," Woodward said.

Should have known, Stevie thought. I write about ballplayers, he writes about presidents. "Well, good luck with it," he said, trying to sound grown-up.

"Thanks," Woodward said as his phone started to ring. He looked at the phone and sighed. "It's Joe Biden. I probably better take it." He waved goodbye as he reached for the phone.

Yeah, Stevie thought, you should probably pick up when the vice president of the United States calls.

Rennie led Stevie, still in a state of semi-shock, through the newsroom to a conference room near the sports area.

A large group, including Bobby, Tamara, and Susan Carol, had gathered. Some were seated, others were pouring coffee and grabbing Danish and bagels from a table in the front of the room.

"Stevie!" Susan Carol called out, racing across the room to give him a hug and a quick kiss. She was dressed Sunday casual—blue jeans and a blouse with a sweater— but Stevie only noticed the boots that added to her height advantage. He almost said, "You had to wear the heels?" but wisely resisted.

"How was your trip in?" he asked.

"Easy," she said. "We had breakfast at Krupin's—you'd have loved it, a real New York deli." Susan Carol knew that Stevie's obsession—beyond sports—was food.

Kelleher and Mearns came over to say hello, and introductions were made around the table once everyone sat down. The meeting was being run by Matt Vita, the *Post's* sports editor, and Tom Goldman, the *Herald's* sports editor. In all there were about twenty people in the room.

"We want a good two weeks of stories in the run-up to the game," Vita said. "Some will be predictable: history of the game, best Army-Navy games ever, rivalry stories, but I want everyone thinking about off-the-beaten-path stories. Camille and Kathy, we're going to lean on you two for ideas since you know Navy so well and can probably offer insight on the Army side too."

Stevie had done some reading yesterday, so he knew that Camille Powell was the *Post's* Navy beat writer and Kathy Orton covered the team for the *Herald*. He also knew that Navy had beaten Rutgers 31–7 on Saturday to raise its record to 8–2. They had one more game left before Army: next week at Notre Dame. Army had played a huge game too, winning at Air Force for—Stevie had gaped when he had read the stat in the paper—only the second time since 1977. The Cadets were also 8–2, with a home game left against Georgia Tech before they played Navy.

Vita and Goldman went around the table doling out assignments and asking for suggestions. "Stevie, Susan Carol, you two are our wild cards," Vita said when it was their turn. "Stevie, since you don't live that far from West Point, we're going to send you up there. You'll go to the Georgia Tech game next week, and then we want you to spend as much time there after that as you can. Susan Carol, we'll send you to South Bend for the Navy–Notre Dame game and then on to Annapolis afterward.

"You're just trying to find interesting story lines regardless of where you are. Susan Carol, since you'll be with Navy, before you get started, get some guidance from Camille and Kathy."

Susan Carol nodded.

"Oh, one more thing for you two," Vita added. "On the Monday before the game, you'll be going to the White House to interview President Obama."

"Really—why us?" Stevie couldn't help asking.

"We thought having the two of you do it might make it more interesting, get him a little off-message. Woodward set it up for us."

Wow, Stevie thought, an interview with the president. Now *that* should make for some interesting reporting.

The meeting lasted a couple hours, and then Stevie, Susan Carol, Kelleher, and Mearns went into Mearns's office to talk more about story ideas. That done, they all went to get a late lunch before dropping Stevie at Union Station for his five o'clock train home again. Stevie's only regret was that he didn't get to spend any time alone with Susan Carol. And since she would be with Navy and he would be with Army, he wouldn't even see her all that much before the game.

When he brought it up, Kelleher smiled and said, "Are you in this to cover sports or to hang out with Susan Carol?"

"Both," Stevie answered.

Mearns laughed. "You have to respect an honest man," she said.

Susan Carol said nothing. But the smile on her face told him he had answered Kelleher's question correctly.

ON THE POST

The next few days dragged for Stevie. School was, quite simply, something he knew he had to do. The only subject that really excited him was history, and this week was more about English, math, and Spanish.

But on Friday he got out of school early so he and Kelleher could drive up to West Point. The Army team would be getting ready to leave campus to spend the night before the game in a hotel.

Kelleher, as usual, had done some advance planning. "They've started a tradition under Coach Ellerson of seeing the team off whenever they leave the Post," Kelleher said. "We'll be there in time for that. And Cantelupe and Noto will meet us. We'll eat dinner in the mess hall so you can get a feel for how the cadets live, and then we'll have to be up early for the game in the morning."

Stevie could fill in most of the blanks Kelleher had left

in his explanation: Rich Ellerson was Army's coach. It was only his second year there, but he had completely turned around a program that had endured twelve straight losing seasons. Jim Cantelupe and Anthony Noto were former Army football players Kelleher had come to know through the years. Cantelupe was some kind of investment banker who lived in Chicago. Noto was the chief financial officer for the NFL. The one thing Stevie didn't understand was Kelleher's reference to "the Post."

Kelleher laughed. "Sorry, it's an Army thing," he said. "The college is on an Army post. A lot more people live and work there than the four thousand cadets. So they call it the Post. At Navy, which is a lot smaller, the campus is called the Yard. There's a lot of Army-Navy lingo—you'll pick it up."

The drive north was pretty, and fortunately traffic was relatively light. By late afternoon, Stevie spotted a sign that said WEST POINT — 2 MILES.

They had to go through two security checkpoints to enter the Post.

"That big building on our right is the Thayer Hotel, which is where we're staying tonight," Kelleher said as they drove up to the second checkpoint. "It's named for Sylvanus Thayer, who founded the academy."

They drove up a hill and Stevie was amazed by the beauty of the place. It was a crisp fall day and the trees were all decked out in reds and golds. Stevie could see the football stadium and water beyond that.

"That's the reservoir," Kelleher said. "Beyond that is

the Hudson River. We'll take a tour tomorrow morning and you'll be able to see it all. It's pretty spectacular."

They took a right turn beyond the stadium, wound around, and Kelleher pulled into a parking lot. "It's not a long walk from here," he said. "We've got a few minutes since we didn't hit much traffic."

They walked through the parking lot and across a street and came to a massive open area. "They call this the Plain," Kelleher said. "It's the central part of the campus. Those bleachers across the way are set up for the parade tomorrow morning." He pointed at a statue. "Sylvanus Thayer," he said.

"Guess he's kind of a star around here," Stevie said.

Kelleher laughed. "I'd say so. But there are lots of statues. In fact, the place we're going has a giant statue of George Washington and we'll also walk past one of Douglas MacArthur."

Stevie's phone was buzzing in his pocket. He looked at the number and answered: it was Susan Carol.

"Where are you?" she asked.

"Walking by a bunch of generals," Stevie said. "How about you?"

"We're on our way to have dinner with the Navy team at the hotel," she said. "We were just at the stadium when the team did their walk-through. What an amazing place it is. Touchdown Jesus is even cooler in person than on TV. Pat Haden was really nice, and so was Tom Hammond, the announcers, you know, from NBC? I guess Tom and Tamara are old friends."

Her words were coming in a rush, her southern accent in full flight.

"Where are you staying?" he said when she paused for breath.

"Oh! That's a funny story too," she said. "We're staying with the team in a place over the Indiana-Michigan state line in a town called Michiana."

"Michigan?"

"Yeah. All the hotels around here require a two-night stay on football weekends—even for the visiting teams. Then they charge like four hundred dollars a night. So the visiting teams stay about forty-five minutes away, over the state line."

"That's crazy," Stevie said.

"Well, when you're Notre Dame, I guess you can get away with it," she said. "Tamara told me the place where y'all are stayin' is great."

"Haven't been there yet. I'll let you know. But the Post is pretty impressive."

"Oh, gotta go. We're pullin' in to the hotel."

"Do I hear a siren?"

"Yes—they let us follow the Navy buses, so there's a police escort with us. Talk soon."

He snapped the phone shut, shaking his head.

"Sounds like she's having fun," Kelleher said, smiling.

"She always has fun. Does anyone ever say no to Tamara or to her?"

"Nope," Kelleher said. "And that includes you and me."

* * *

Anthony Noto and Jim Cantelupe looked like the ex–football players they were. Neither was that big, but both had broad shoulders and seemed like they were still in playing shape to Stevie, even though Noto was class of '91, Cantelupe class of '96.

The two Army grads walked Kelleher and Stevie over to a spot not far from the statue of George Washington. As they got there, the giant doors of the building just beyond the statue opened and cadets began pouring out of them, most of them screaming and waving their arms. For a second, Stevie thought they had walked into the middle of a full-scale riot.

"They assemble inside the mess hall, then race out here to get into formation just before the team arrives," Noto explained. "It used to be we only did stuff like this the week of the Navy game. But Coach Ellerson wants to send the message that every game's a big game and that the corps needs to be behind the team every week. So he started this send-off when he got here."

"Actually, I think they've done something like this for years," Cantelupe said. "At least for road games."

While they were talking, most of the cadets were organizing themselves into rows; each of them seemed to know exactly where to stand. One group had broken off and had formed an alley of sorts that led to a walkway between the two buildings.

"Plebes," Noto said, and seeing Stevie's expression

added, "Freshmen. They form the cordon the players will walk through. Then the team assembles over here. And the buses are waiting for them over there."

At that moment a loud cheer went up and Stevie saw what had to be the football team, even though they were dressed in neat gray uniforms like everyone else. The plebes were going crazy cheering. The upperclassmen were joining in, though not quite as enthusiastically as the first-year cadets.

Once everyone had walked through the cordon, the players assembled in front of the statue. Coach Rich Ellerson stepped to a microphone.

"We aren't going to take long," he said, "but I want you all to know how much it means to us to see you assembled out here."

"As if they had any choice," Kelleher whispered.

"I think at Navy they call it 'mandatory fun,'" Cantelupe said.

Ellerson was still talking. "We're playing a team tomorrow that has great athletes. We're playing a team coached by a man who *used* to coach at Navy."

Boos erupted when Georgia Tech coach Paul Johnson's ties to Navy were mentioned.

Ellerson held his hands up for quiet. "A man who was *six and oh* against Army while at Navy."

The boos got considerably louder.

"Tomorrow, we're going to show Coach Johnson and his players that Army football isn't what it used to be! We're going to show him what Army football is *now* and give his team a beating it won't forget anytime soon! But we need *your* help! You are the twelfth man! Do *not* let down for one second tomorrow in the stands. I promise you we will *not* let down for one second on the field!"

The cadets were whipped into a frenzy, and suddenly— or so it seemed to Stevie—the band appeared and began playing the Army fight song, "On, Brave Old Army Team." Stevie knew a lot of college fight songs, and this was one of the best ones going. With the whole corps singing, he couldn't help but get caught up in the energy of the moment.

When the final words of the song died away, the en- tire corps—all four thousand of them—finished with two words: "BEAT NAVY!"

Then everyone surged forward to offer the players handshakes and pats on the back as they headed for the buses.

Kelleher nudged Stevie. "So?"

"Oh yeah," Stevie said. "This is going to be fun."

They ate in the mess hall, which was huge and filled with a sea of gray uniforms. People kept stopping to say hello to Cantelupe and Noto, who were obviously still well known at their alma mater. Cadets kept walking by the table say- ing, "Good evening, sir," to everyone in sight. The food wasn't very good, but there was plenty of it, which worked for Stevie.

While they ate, Kelleher asked Cantelupe and Noto to give Stevie some background on Army football.

"It started in 1890, when a cadet named Dennis Michie got some guys together and challenged Navy to a game," Noto said. "Football was a new sport back then, a lot different than today. . . ."

"Anthony, can we fast-forward a little?" Kelleher said. "We really haven't got time for one hundred and twenty years of history."

Cantelupe jumped in. "You know how Anthony is: ask him how Roger Goodell's feeling and he'll tell you the life history of the NFL."

"Funny," Noto said, but he was smiling.

"I think what Stevie should know is how Army football—actually football at Army, Navy, and Air Force—is different than at civilian schools."

"Civilian schools?" Stevie asked.

Cantelupe nodded. "Basically any other college you can name. You're from Philadelphia, right? Villanova, Temple, Penn, they're all civilian schools.

"Every single student at Army, Navy, and Air Force is on a full scholarship—paid for by the government," he continued. "And in return, every one of them will go into the military for five years when they graduate."

"Five years?" Stevie said.

"Uh-huh," Cantelupe said. "That's why you won't see a lot of NFL prospects on these teams. Five years in the military after college will pretty much end your chances of playing in the pros. Roger Staubach was the major exception to that rule. He fought in Vietnam in the sixties before he played for the Cowboys. There have been a few others, but not many."

Noto picked up from there. "That doesn't mean the academies don't care about football or try to recruit players. They do. In fact, unlike the civilian schools, they don't have scholarship limits. A civilian school can only have eighty-five players on football scholarships at any one time. The academies can recruit as many guys as they want—as long as they can get into school academically. Most years, about a hundred plebes will show up for the first day of football practice. Four years later, if there are twenty or twenty-five of them still playing, that's a lot.

"Recruiting's tough, because you have to find a kid who can not only play football but also make it at the academy. If a student comes here and hates the military life or can't cut it in class, he'll be gone. So one of the keys to success for the academies is having a low attrition rate—the fewer players you lose, especially the first two years when they have plenty of opportunity to transfer, the better off you'll be. This team has twenty-three seniors. Last year's only had nine. It makes a big difference."

Stevie was digging into some ice cream as Cantelupe and Noto continued their lesson when he heard a voice from above saying, "May I have the attention of the corps?"

Stevie looked up and saw a cadet standing on a platform in the middle of the room.

Seeing his puzzled look, Noto said, "That's called the

poop deck. It's where announcements are made at the end of meals and where visitors are introduced."

Sure enough, the cadet welcomed Cantelupe and Noto back, to big cheers from the student body. Then the announcer went on. "As everyone knows, tomorrow's game will be televised by ESPN." More cheering broke out.

"These guys will cheer for just about anything, won't they?" Kelleher said, smiling.

"They don't get much chance most days," Cantelupe said.

"We'd like to introduce the announcers for the game," the cadet went on. "Brent Musburger will do play-by-play." (Cheers.) "Kirk Herbstreit will do color." (More cheers.) "And Jack Arute will be the sideline reporter." (Moans, no doubt, Stevie thought, because they were hoping for one of the good-looking women ESPN employed to do sideline reporting.)

Musburger made a predictable speech: it was an honor to be back at West Point, he was thrilled with the job Coach Ellerson and his young men were doing. . . .

As he droned on, Stevie noticed a man in a sharp-looking dark suit approaching the table. Kelleher seemed to notice him at the same moment and waved. "Hey, Pete, over here," he said in a stage whisper as Musburger continued.

"The courage all of you show every single day makes me proud to be an American. . . ."

Pete and Kelleher hugged hello and sat down as Herbstreit was taking the microphone.

"I'm a proud graduate of Ohio State University," he began. "But nothing would make me more proud than to have one of my children attend West Point. . . ."

As the cadets cheered, Kelleher introduced his friend.

"Pete Dowling, special agent, United States Secret Service, meet Anthony Noto, Jim Cantelupe, and Steve Thomas."

Dowling shook hands around the table while Herbstreit passed the microphone to Jack Arute and the cadets began to boo him good-naturedly.

Arute held his hands up as if to say, "I know, I know." He shook his head. "I'm sorry I'm not Erin Andrews," he said as more mock boos filled the air. "Would it help to tell you that I *know* Erin Andrews?"

The answer was apparently no. Arute, after apologizing several more times for not being blond or female, wrapped up his remarks by saying he had never looked forward to an assignment more than this one. And at last everyone could go back to finishing dessert.

"So, Pete, what brings you here?" Noto asked.

"I had a meeting with the superintendent," Dowling said. "Just doing some prep work for the president's appearance at Army-Navy. Bobby and I are old friends, and he let me know he'd be on Post, so here I am."

"Actually, Stevie, I wanted you to meet Pete. He's going to be your contact with the Secret Service leading up to the game. Susan Carol will be working with another agent who is handling the Navy people. Security is one story we want you guys to do before the game."

Dowling nodded. "There are some things I can't tell you, Steve, but I'll fill you in on what we do to prepare for something like this."

"So it's a big deal?" Stevie asked.

"Any time the president travels, it's a big deal," Dowling said. "When he's traveling to a stadium with ninety thousand people inside, it's way beyond a big deal."

"So what'd you talk to the supe about?" Cantelupe asked.

"Mostly logistics and paperwork," Dowling answered. "We've got to get IDs and run background checks on every player, coach, trainer, manager, you name it, who will be on the field with the president. We'll also run ID checks on every cadet and every midshipman before they march onto the field."

"Yeah, that's one thing you need to watch," Cantelupe said.

Dowling looked at him for a moment to see if he was joking and seemed to decide he wasn't. "What do you mean?"

Cantelupe looked a little embarrassed. "When I was a plebe, a buddy of mine from back home wanted to go to the game, but I'd used up all my tickets," he said. "So I loaned him one of my uniforms—we were about the same size—and he marched on with the cadets."

"And no one picked up on it?" Dowling asked.

Cantelupe shook his head. "The guys in my company knew what was going on, but they didn't care; they thought it was kind of funny."

Dowling shook his head, clearly pained. "Not funny with the president there," he said. "That's one angle I hadn't thought about. I guess now I'll have to."

"Some kid in a cadet uniform is hardly a problem, is it?" Kelleher said.

"Not a problem at all," Dowling said. "Unless he's not just some kid."

"Ah," Kelleher said. "Sounds like you've got your work cut out for you."

Dowling shrugged. "In one sense, it's routine—we're trained on how to prepare for both big and small events. In another sense, it's never routine when the president leaves the White House."

"Do you get a lot of threats?" Stevie asked.

Dowling nodded. "All the time," he said. "Especially with this president because there are still some idiots who can't deal with the idea of an African American being president. But we don't really worry about those much."

"Why not?" Stevie asked.

"Because," Dowling said, "if you really want to attack the president, you don't tell the people protecting him that you're planning to do it."

GAME DAY: 2 HOURS, 26 MINUTES TO KICKOFF

Stevie's first thought when Pete Dowling said they had to go get a gun was that, for some reason, he didn't have his own gun. He could see the shoulder holster inside his jacket but not the actual gun.

"No, I've got it," Dowling said as they walked off the field, opening his jacket so Stevie could see the gun inside the holster. "I'd actually be breaking the law if I was on duty and not wearing it. But only Secret Service agents are armed today. *No one* else carries any kind of weapon into the stadium."

"Not even the local police?" Stevie asked.

"Nope," Dowling said. "Anyone who is armed is work-ing outside. We're after a different kind of gun—one that the officials will use to signal the end of each quarter."

"Really? I thought there was a horn or that the refs blew their whistles," said Stevie.

"Yes, you're right, most teams have switched to that. But *not* Army-Navy. Because of the military tradition, they still shoot a gun, and at the end of the game they fire a cannon."

"So where do we go?" Stevie asked.

"Come on, I'll show you."

They walked outside the stadium, causing Stevie to wonder if he would have to endure another prolonged security check when they went back inside. There were several unmarked trailers in this corner of the parking lot, each with someone who was wearing the Secret Service "uniform"—dark suit, sunglasses, wire coming out of one ear—posted at the entrances.

Dowling walked up to one of the trailers, and the agent posted at the bottom of the steps wordlessly moved aside for him and for Stevie. Dowling was more effective than an all-access pass.

The trailer was full of agents sitting at computers, sipping coffee, talking on cell phones. Stevie followed Dowling into a back room, where an attractive woman was seated at a computer.

"Grace, meet Steve Thomas," Dowling said. "He's the young reporter I told you about. Steve, this is Grace Andrade."

Grace Andrade stood up to say hello. She looked the way Stevie imagined Susan Carol might look in twenty years: tall and athletic with long, dark hair and a great smile. "I live here in Washington, so I've been reading what you and Ms. Anderson have been writing all week," she said. "Very impressive."

"Thank you," Stevie said. "We've had a lot of help. We appreciate getting to shadow the Secret Service."

"You got the gun?" Dowling asked.

"Right here," Grace said, picking up a small handgun that had been sitting next to the computer and handing it to Dowling.

He flipped the cylinder open so Stevie could see inside. "There are four blanks loaded in there."

"Hypothetically," Stevie asked. "Let's say one of the refs was crazy. Couldn't he have bullets in his pocket?"

"He'd never get them inside the stadium today with the metal detectors," Dowling said. "Plus, you've seen how we sweep the stadium for anything suspicious before the game, so he couldn't hide them in advance either. And third, notice how the inside has been soldered? This gun can't be loaded with anything but blanks."

"So you're like everyone else," Stevie said. "You don't trust the referees."

Dowling laughed. "I'm different from everyone else," he said. "I don't trust *anyone*."

They thanked Grace, left the trailer, and walked back inside the stadium. Dowling waved off the security people, saying, "He's already been checked," as they passed the screening area.

To Stevie it seemed like there were cops and agents everywhere he looked. This early in the day, their numbers rivaled those of the fans.

"So how many guys are working with you on this?" Stevie asked.

"That I can't tell you. Or how many women, either," Dowling answered with a grin. "We don't release staffing numbers because we don't want anyone to know for sure what they might be up against or where a potential weak spot might be.

"But I can say that we've had Secret Service agents, stadium security, and local police from all the surrounding counties working together on the pregame clearances, as well as the game-day security."

They walked through the hallways of the stadium, Dowling taking him on a tour of every locker room in the building. Squads of officers with bomb-sniffing dogs had checked the locker rooms where the teams, the bands, and the cheerleaders would be. Agents in special gloves checked every locker and every office and filing cabinet. As more agents checked in with Dowling, Stevie found the scale of the job more and more staggering.

They were heading in the direction of a sign that said REDSKINS LOCKER ROOM when Stevie saw a group of policemen with bomb dogs, rent-a-cops, and two men in suits standing outside. One suit had a walkie-talkie, and the other was clearly an agent.

"Hey, Pete," the agent said. "We were about to call you. We've got a little problem."

Dowling raised an eyebrow.

"Dude in the suit with the walkie is claiming he hasn't been given clearance by 'Mr. Snyder' to let anyone in the locker room."

"You're joking," Dowling said.

"I wish I was."

"You explained to him that we're in total control of this building until the president leaves here today?"

"I did. He said, 'Only Mr. Snyder is in charge of this building at all times.'"

Dowling rolled his eyes. He looked at his watch. "Well, we made it to ten o'clock before we encountered our first real idiot. Not bad, considering."

He walked to the man in the suit, with Stevie a step and a half behind, wanting to hear without crowding Dowling.

"What do you want?" the man said to Dowling.

Dowling pulled out his wallet and flashed his badge. "My name is Peter Dowling. I'm the agent in charge of this detail. My men need to get in this locker room and they need to get in *right now.*"

The man started to say something, but Dowling cut him off. "The president of the United States is going to be here in less than two hours, so I don't have time for discussion. If you don't get this door open in thirty seconds, you will be charged with interfering with the United States Secret Service."

The dude's tough look had faded. "Look, give me a minute to check with my boss," he said, starting to raise his walkie-talkie to his mouth.

"*I'm* your boss right now," Dowling said. "Twenty seconds."

"Okay, okay," the man said. He reached in his pocket for some keys and Stevie could see his hands were shaking. "I know I'll get in trouble with Mr. Snyder for this."

"Better him than me," Dowling said. "What do you think the chances are that Mr. Snyder would come bail you out of jail?"

The man got the locker room door open. Dowling waved the cops with the dogs inside and told the other agent that everything else on this level was clear. When the man tried to follow them inside, Dowling stepped in front of him.

"That's off-limits to everyone except people we authorize to go inside. Once we've cleared the room, you can stay outside and continue to guard it with your usual diligence."

He turned to Stevie. "Come on, we've got a delivery to make."

Stevie had kinda wanted to see Dowling put the dude in handcuffs, but he followed him down the hall.

"We'll drop off the starter's gun and go back on the field." Dowling paused for a moment to talk into his wrist. "Mike, are the officials here?" he asked.

"That's a yes," he heard a voice say faintly.

"Their room has been checked and cleared? And their escort to and from the field is set, right?" Dowling said.

"Roger."

They rounded a corner and came upon a room with a

sign that said NO ONE WITHOUT THE AUTHORITY OF THE NATIONAL FOOTBALL LEAGUE MAY ENTER AT ANY TIME. . . .

An agent on the door smiled as they walked up. He knocked to alert the officials, then opened the door so Dowling and Stevie could enter.

The officials' locker room was bigger than most basketball locker rooms Stevie had been in. The seven officials were all in their uniforms, and an eighth man, in sweats, was standing in the back of the room.

The man nearest the door approached when Dowling walked in.

"Agent Dowling?" he said. "We talked on the phone. I'm Mike Daniels. I'm the referee today."

"Nice to meet you," Dowling said. "I know you've met my partner, Bob Campbell, out at Notre Dame. This is Steve Thomas with the *Washington Herald*. He's observing."

"We've met," Daniels said, refusing to look Stevie in the eye. It hadn't been a pleasant meeting and Stevie found himself starting to sweat a little, but if Dowling noticed, he didn't say anything.

"Who's this?" Dowling said, nodding in the direction of the guy in the sweats.

"Oh, that's Todd—he takes care of our locker room and locks up after us when we go on the field."

"First I heard of it," Dowling said.

"I got cleared by your people," Todd said. "Sent in my Social Security number and all that good stuff."

"You work for the Redskins?" Dowling asked.

Todd shook his head. "No. Actually, I'm Mike's

nephew. He brings me along on his trips to do all the locker room stuff. One of the Redskins guys showed me around yesterday."

"Good," Dowling said. "You mind stepping outside a minute?"

Todd looked at his uncle, who turned to Dowling. "If Todd leaves, then the kid leaves too, right?"

"No," Dowling said. "He's writing a story on pregame security and I've authorized him to be here. Is there a problem?"

"I'm not a big fan of the media," Daniels mumbled.

"That's your issue, not mine," Dowling said.

Daniels didn't look pleased, but he nodded at Todd, who walked to the door.

Once Todd was gone, Daniels introduced the rest of his crew—two line judges, the umpire, and the three back judges. Most of the names flew past Stevie except that of one line judge—Terry Ramspeth. When they were introduced, Ramspeth gave him a look and said, "You work with that girl, don't you?"

"You mean Susan Carol Anderson?" Stevie said.

"Yeah. I was on the crew at Notre Dame. So were Paul, Zach, and of course Mike. We really didn't appreciate what she wrote about us."

"Yeah, Mr. Daniels has made that pretty clear on a couple of occasions," Stevie said.

"She basically called us cheats," said Paul Lynch, the umpire.

Before Stevie could respond, Dowling held up a hand.

"Gentlemen, there's no time for this right now," he said. "Let's focus on the game at hand, shall we?"

Dowling pulled the starter's gun from his jacket pocket. "Mike, you're in charge of this, right?"

Daniels nodded. Dowling showed him the four blanks and how the loading mechanism had been disabled. "Keep this with you at all times," he said. "If it shows up in someone else's hands, you're responsible."

"That's fine," Daniels said. "It can't hurt anyone, can it?"

"No, it can't. But it could scare the hell out of people—especially with the president around. We don't need it going off by accident at the wrong time and creating havoc."

"Got it," Daniels said.

He shook hands with Dowling.

"Hey, kid, do us a favor," the umpire said to Stevie. "If we do a good job today, if we're fair to both teams, you be fair too and write something nice about us. Tell the whole story. Okay?"

Stevie thought that was a pretty reasonable request.

"You got it," he said, and the man nodded. Daniels was still glaring at him. Clearly they weren't going to shake and make up. Stevie followed Dowling out the door.

The last of the thirty-two companies of Army cadets were entering the field as Stevie and Dowling rejoined the others on the sidelines.

"They *do* march better," Stevie commented.

There was something just a little crisper and more precise about the cadets than the midshipmen. He had thought Kelleher was exaggerating and probably *was* an Army fan, but now he could see what he meant.

When all the cadets were in place on the field, they snapped to a salute as one, and the PA announcer said:

"Ladies and gentlemen, standing before you are the cadets of the United States Military Academy and members of the U.S. Army Cadet Command. Every one of them has chosen to answer the call to duty. With their salute, they recognize and honor your show of support. These cadets today will lead American sons and daughters tomorrow in defense of our great nation."

After rousing applause, the cadets began to march off the field and into their seats.

Stevie could see that the stadium had filled up quickly. Soon the teams would come out to go through their pregame warm-ups.

Susan Carol asked Stevie, "So how'd it go with the gun?"

"Fine. Daniels will be carrying it. Lucky for you, it only shoots blanks."

Susan Carol blanched. Stevie could joke about it, but her ongoing conflict with the officials had shaken her up more than she cared to admit. Even with all the scandals she and Stevie had broken, she'd never had a story come back at her the way her story on the officials had. She'd never felt such an outpouring of venom. Worse was that she couldn't quite shake the feeling that maybe they had a right to be mad at her. That in the heat of writing her story about the Navy–Notre Dame game, she had let her emotions carry her too far.

THE MIDSHIPMEN

Susan Carol and Tamara were at dinner in a private dining room with the Navy team on the night before the Notre Dame game. Having been around NFL players in the past, Susan Carol was amazed at the size—or lack of it—of the Navy players.

"Where are all the linemen?" she asked Tamara as they stood in the buffet line.

"I'm a lineman, ma'am," the player in front of her said.

Every player they had been introduced to so far had called Susan Carol "ma'am." She knew she looked older than fourteen, but the players had to know she was younger than they were. And yet she kept getting called "ma'am."

"I'm Susan Carol Anderson," she said, putting out her hand. "And I'm only fourteen, so you don't have to call me 'ma'am.' Are you really a lineman?"

The player smiled. "Yes, ma'am, I am. I'm Garrett Smith, and I start at offensive tackle. It's nice to meet you."

"How much do you weigh, Garrett?" Susan Carol asked. For a normal human being, the player was huge, but for a college football lineman at the highest level, he was tiny—barely taller than she was. She had read the Notre Dame media guide on the way out and had noticed that the *smallest* starting offensive lineman weighed 305 pounds.

Garrett Smith smiled at the question. "Well, once I'm through eating here, I hope to weigh two sixty-five."

"So why'd you choose Navy, Garrett?" Susan Carol asked as they picked up plates. "Were you recruited anywhere else?"

"Oh, lots of places," Smith said. "Dartmouth, Yale, Holy Cross. Williams and Wesleyan really wanted me."

Those were all great academic schools, but none played powerhouse football.

"Well," Smith amended, "I recruited Dartmouth and Yale. They said they'd let me try out if I went there."

"You must be a good student," Susan Carol said.

"Pretty good," Smith answered.

"How good is pretty good?"

Smith was now filling his plate with as much pasta and chicken as could possibly fit on it.

"My GPA is 3.87."

"Yeah, I'd say that's pretty good," Susan Carol said. "What's your major?"

"Thermonuclear engineering."

Susan Carol couldn't help but laugh. She knew she

was in a different world than the one that existed at the big-time football schools. She thought back to the Final Four when she and Stevie had rolled their eyes at the press conference moderators who kept referring to all the players as "student-athletes," even though fewer than forty percent of the starters on teams that made the tournament ever graduated. At Navy—and she was pretty sure at Army too—the players really were "student-athletes."

After she and Tamara had gotten their food, Susan Carol saw Coach Ken Niumatalolo waving them over to his table.

"Must be getting close to Army-Navy," he said with a smile, giving Tamara a friendly hug. "Is this the young lady that Kathy and Camille told me about?"

Tamara nodded. "Susan Carol Anderson, this is Ken Niumatalolo, a lovely man with an impossible-to-spell name."

"Just write 'Niumat,'" Niumatalolo said. "Or, even better, write more about the kids and less about me."

They sat down and Niumatalolo introduced some of the coaches around the table, including Ivin Jasper, the offensive coordinator, and Buddy Green, who was in charge of the defense.

"Susan Carol just got her first sense of what makes a Navy football player," Tamara said. "She met Garrett Smith."

Niumatalolo laughed. "Honestly, when I tell other coaches at the civilian schools about our players, they don't believe me," he said. "They can't believe that kids who work this hard academically—not to mention the military training—can compete the way they do. We've got twelve plebes on this trip. They've all had watch at some point this week." Susan Carol looked confused, so he explained, "It means they have to stay up all night and watch some portion of the Yard—which is our campus. With most of our opponents, if a player is up all night, it's because he's at a party."

"Don't forget six-weekers," Jasper said.

"Yeah, true," Niumatalolo said. "On our academic calendar, students take tests every six weeks. The only reason we'll have a curfew tonight is because we don't want the guys staying up all night to study."

The more she heard, the more Susan Carol understood why Tamara and Bobby Kelleher thought this game was so special.

"I can't wait to get to know the team better," Susan Carol said.

"You'll get your chance," Niumatalolo said. "But first let's see if we can beat the Irish."

After dinner, Susan Carol was introduced to Matt Klunder, who was apparently the number-two man at the academy. He was young for someone so high up, probably in his forties, she guessed.

"Captain Klunder's the commandant," Tamara said. "That means he's in charge of the day-to-day lives of the midshipmen."

"Except when there's a really tough decision to make," Klunder said. "Then I take it to the supe."

The supe—superintendent—was Vice Admiral Jeffrey Fowler. Klunder explained he would fly in the next morning. "I think he's bringing the SecNav with him," Klunder said. Susan Carol was beginning to realize that these people didn't really speak English. They spoke Navy.

"SecNav?" she said.

"Sorry," Klunder said. "The secretary of the Navy."

"So, Matt, can we watch from the sidelines tomorrow?" Tamara asked.

"Well, that's where I'll be," Klunder said. "If you can take the cold, you're both welcome."

"We'll handle it," Tamara said.

"You'd make a good mid," Klunder said, laughing.

"No thanks," Tamara said. "I don't think I want to do push-ups every time you guys score."

"Let's hope we do a lot of them tomorrow," Klunder said.

The minute they walked outside the hotel the next morning, Susan Carol didn't think Tamara's sideline idea was a good one. Not only was it cold, it was snowing sideways.

Tamara had offered a ride to the two Navy radio announcers, Bob Socci and Omar Nelson, and the four of them hurried to the car.

"We're going to freeze to death on the sidelines," Susan Carol said.

"It's not so bad," Socci said.

"Feels bad to me," Susan Carol said.

"That's because you're from North Carolina," Tamara said. "You think fifty is cold."

"Fifty *is* cold," Susan Carol said as they all climbed in.

It took them almost an hour to get to the Notre Dame campus. "We'll go up to the press box to stay warm for a little while," Tamara said. "Then we'll go downstairs."

"I can't wait," Susan Carol said.

"You can always watch the game from our booth," Socci said. "It'll be toasty warm in there."

"No, she can't," Tamara said. "She's here to get to know what it's like to be a Navy football player, not what it's like to be a Navy broadcaster."

They took the elevator up to the press box, which *was* toasty warm. Susan Carol was sipping a cup of coffee and talking to Tom Hammond and Pat Haden, the NBC broadcasters, when Tamara—who had gone to get their sideline passes—came back with a man dressed in a dark suit.

"This is Bob Campbell, from the Secret Service."

Stevie had mentioned meeting a Secret Service agent when they'd spoken last night, but Campbell had an easy smile that belied his serious job.

"Hey, Bob, any chance our sideline reporter might grab you for a minute during the game?" Hammond said. "Might be something a little different for our viewers."

Campbell shook his head. "I'm sorry," he said. "We aren't allowed to do interviews."

"But you can talk to Tamara and Susan Carol?" Haden asked.

"On background only," Campbell said. "If I'm quoted in a story, I'm in trouble."

All too soon it was time to head to the field, and Campbell joined Susan Carol and Tamara in the elevator.

"So, on background," Susan Carol said. "What exactly are you out here for?"

Campbell smiled. "Last night I met with some of the Navy people to explain what the game-day procedures will be. Most of them have done this before, so they're prepared. I also got introduced to the players during their evening meeting to explain what we'll need from them in terms of background checks and what it will be like on game day. I also like to be around and for the players to know who I am so if there are any problems at all, they can come to me."

"Yes—doesn't one of them know you too well?" Tamara asked. "Who was the kid the service thought was a fugitive a couple years ago?"

"Ram Vela." Campbell shook his head. "His full name is Ramiro Ray Vela, which is the exact same name of a fugitive we were looking for. When the team came to the White House to accept the Commander-in-Chief's Trophy, our guys pulled him in, thinking he might be the guy. Of course he wasn't."

"I need to talk to *him*," Susan Carol said.

"Thanks for bringing it up, Tamara," Campbell said. "But you'll like him, Susan Carol. He's a pretty good linebacker for a guy who is about five foot nine."

"A linebacker who is shorter than I am?" Susan Carol said.

"Noticeably shorter," Campbell answered.

They had reached the tunnel that led to the field. As they were walking past the Notre Dame locker room, she heard a voice say, "Clear the way, clear the way."

She looked behind her and saw Brian Kelly, the Notre Dame coach, surrounded by a coterie of security people. One of them, walking in front of Kelly, was waving his arms to make sure no one got within shouting distance of the coach.

"Clear out!" he barked as Susan Carol and Tamara stepped back to avoid being stampeded. Campbell wasn't quite as quick, though, and one of the man's swinging hands caught him on the shoulder.

"Watch it, pal," the security guard barked.

"Oh my, this could get ugly," Susan Carol hissed to Tamara.

Campbell seemed almost not to react to the smack on the shoulder or the rude tone in the guard's voice.

As Kelly swept by, he calmly put his hand on the guard's shoulder. "Got a minute?" he said quietly.

The guard gave him a look. "You with NBC or something?" he said, perhaps assuming someone in a suit worked for TV.

Campbell shook his head and produced his wallet for a split second. "Secret Service," he said. "I know a little about protection. Let me give you a word of advice: the fewer people that notice you, the better."

"What's the Secret Service doing at Notre Dame?" the guard asked.

"Can't tell you," Campbell said. "Classified." Then he walked back to join Tamara and Susan Carol. The guard said nothing.

"He was so rude," Susan Carol said. "For a minute, I thought you'd arrest him."

Campbell shrugged. "I think I made my point. Probably should have just let it go."

They made their way onto the field, where the teams were warming up. The snow had slacked off, but it was still cold and windy. As she followed Campbell and Tamara to the sideline, Susan Carol felt a tap on her shoulder.

"You sure you want to watch from here?" a voice said.

She turned and saw Ken Niumatalolo, who had a big smile on his face. He had somehow made it all the way from his locker room to the 50-yard line without the aid of eight security people.

"You're from Hawaii," Susan Carol said. "Is this weather killing you too?"

"Can't stand it," Niumatalolo replied. "But once the game starts, I swear I won't even notice it."

The teams left the field a few minutes later and the Notre Dame band marched on, playing the famous fight song "Cheer, Cheer for Old Notre Dame." With the eighty-thousand-seat stadium now almost full and the fight song blaring, Susan Carol had to admit—this was a pretty amazing place to watch the game.

And the game was so good Susan Carol almost forgot how cold she was. Notre Dame's record was 7–2, and they were still hoping to get into one of the bowl games that paid huge money to the participating teams. She had read a story about how Notre Dame had removed a lot of its tougher games from its schedule to try to get some easy wins. Navy was an annual game that Notre Dame had won forty-three years in a row, from 1963 through 2006. But Navy had won two of the last three games, which was probably one of the reasons Charlie Weis had been fired as coach and replaced by Kelly.

"Why did Navy play these guys all those years when they were losing?" she asked Tamara. "It was like scheduling an automatic loss."

"Well," Tamara said, "the school makes a lot of money on the game, usually about a million dollars. And the players *want* to take on Notre Dame. I was here when they finally broke the losing streak in '07, and the feeling after that game was like nothing I'd ever seen in my life. They love getting this chance."

That became evident during the game. The Navy players were constantly alive, chattering at one another, encouraging the players who were on the field, seemingly never discouraged regardless of what was happening.

And things didn't start well for the Midshipmen. Notre Dame took the opening kickoff and marched smartly down the field. On third down and goal from the 1-yard line, quarterback Roger Valdiserri dropped back and simply threw the ball up in the air toward the corner of the end zone. Two Navy defenders were there covering Irish wide receiver Tom Bates.

But Bates was several inches taller than they were and had a vertical leap that would have served him well on the basketball court. He jumped high above the two Navy players, corralled the ball, and came down with both feet just in bounds.

"This is the whole problem when we play these guys," Susan Carol heard someone say behind her. "They have at least a dozen guys who will play in the NFL. And we have guys who will be deploying to Afghanistan."

Susan Carol turned in the direction of the voice and saw a man who could have outleaped Tom Bates: David Robinson, the Hall of Fame basketball player who was also a Navy graduate. Since Susan Carol was just a shade under six feet tall, she wasn't accustomed to having to look up at people. Robinson, who was easily seven feet, was an exception.

"Susan Carol Anderson, meet David Robinson," Tamara said while the Notre Dame fight song blared after the extra point had been kicked.

"Wow," Susan Carol said, inadvertently using one of Stevie's favorite words. "It's a pleasure to meet you, Mr. Robinson."

"It's David," Robinson said, looking down and shaking her hand. "I know who you are. I remember when you and your friend helped out a couple years ago at the Final Four."

"Did you come in just for the game?" Susan Carol asked.

"I was in Chicago doing a talk, and the Navy people asked if I'd come and speak to the team after the game," he said.

"Why aren't you up in the supe's box, where it's nice and warm?" Tamara asked.

Robinson shook his head. "Have to show the boys my support," he said. "I can deal with the cold."

The boys could have used him on the field most of the first half. Navy simply couldn't get anything going on offense, although the defense did finally get its feet underneath it after Notre Dame's first two touchdowns.

Finally, late in the first half, Navy began to move the ball. A perfectly timed pitch from quarterback Ricky Dobbs to slotback G. G. Greene produced a big play; Greene got a good block on the corner that sprung him for a thirty-nine-yard gain to the Notre Dame 32. The Navy bench exploded as Greene raced down the sideline.

"We need seven before halftime," Robinson said. "We get the ball to start the second half."

Then Dobbs surprised the Irish with a pass over the middle to wide receiver Mike Schupp, who carried the ball to the 11. Running the option offense, Navy rarely passed, but with the clock winding down to a minute, Dobbs took the chance. Two plays later, with just fourteen seconds left, fullback Alex Murray bulled into the end zone behind a great block from Garrett Smith. Suddenly, it was a game, 14–7 at the half.

NO EXCUSES

Right as halftime began, Captain Klunder appeared. He was in his dress uniform and looked a lot less casual than the night before.

"Come on, you three," he said, grabbing Robinson by the arm. "Let's go inside the locker room and get warm."

They followed the players through the tunnel. The security guard did a double take when he saw Robinson and a triple take when he saw Susan Carol and Tamara.

"Admiral, we don't allow women in the locker rooms at Notre Dame," he said to Klunder.

"It's Captain," Klunder said. "And right now this isn't Notre Dame's locker room, it's Navy's. So I'll decide who is and isn't allowed."

The security guard eyed Klunder for a moment but said nothing. Klunder led them all to an office off the locker room where there was hot chocolate, coffee, bottled water, and donuts.

"Help yourselves," Klunder said. "The coaches will meet for a few minutes, and then each position coach will talk to his guys before Kenny talks to the team as a group.

"Hot chocolate, Susan Carol? You look frozen."

"Actually, I'd love some coffee," Susan Carol said, realizing she had drawn out the word *love* to be "lovvvvv" in a way that Stevie would have teased her about.

Klunder gave her a disapproving look. "Aren't you fourteen?" he said.

She sighed. "Yes, but I'm a fourteen-year-old swimmer who's up at five most mornings. Plus, I'm not really worried about stunting my growth."

Klunder laughed and poured her some coffee.

"We're going to win this game," Klunder said, tossing away his napkin. "Our guys have figured them out."

"Easy, Matt," Tamara said. "Remember where you are."

"What do you mean? Luck of the Irish?" Robinson said.

"More like refs of the Irish," Tamara said.

"Oh—too true. Do you remember that line judge?" Klunder said.

"What?" Susan Carol asked.

"Right!" Tamara said. "That was the worst call. . . . Susan Carol, this is years ago—back in '99, I think. Navy had the game won. They stopped Notre Dame a full yard short on fourth down with a minute to go, and Notre Dame was out of time-outs. Then the line judge walked in, picked up the ball, moved it up a yard, and they made the first down by an inch."

"Even in '07, when we won, they threw that mystery flag during the third overtime," Klunder said.

"I remember that," Tamara said.

After a while, they could hear shouts coming from the locker room. They walked into the main room and saw players huddling around various coaches, each of whom had some kind of board to draw x's and o's on while they talked. Every once in a while someone would shout something, clearly in an adrenaline rush, but Susan Carol noticed one phrase repeated frequently.

"Our way of life against theirs!"

"What does that mean?" she asked.

Robinson smiled. "You go to a military academy, you live a distinctly different kind of life than kids who go to a civilian school. It's kind of a rallying cry about being disciplined and tough."

Niumatalolo walked in. "Everybody up," he said in a clear, loud voice, and all the players moved to the middle of the room, where he was standing.

"Fellas, we were a little intimidated at the beginning," he said. "Not sure why, but it doesn't matter. We're every bit as good as these guys on both sides of the ball. If we go out and stay focused and don't let anything distract us, we'll win the game. I told you if we played Navy football, we'd win. You should be more certain now than ever that that's true. Let's go!"

The players pushed themselves into a circle with their hands all in and on the count of three shouted, "Better than the Irish!" and then began charging for the doors. Susan Carol was a little less eager. She wanted to stay warm.

The second half started just like the first—except Navy was the team in control. Alex Teich returned the kickoff to the 43, and from there the Mids' offense was near perfect. Dobbs was making all the right decisions at quarterback: If he put the ball in Murray's stomach, a hole was open in front of him. If he faked, the Irish still went for Murray and he got to the edge for good yardage. Without passing the ball once, Navy went fifty-seven yards in nine plays, Dobbs following a Murray block into the end zone from the 2-yard line. The extra point made it 14–14.

"Now it's a ball game!" Robinson said.

Notre Dame picked up one first down but stalled and had to punt.

Navy immediately launched another drive and picked up a first down at the Notre Dame 18 as the third quarter ended.

"I like all the running plays," Susan Carol said. "Makes the game go faster."

"I like them too," Robinson said, "because they're working."

Navy ran two fullback plunges up the middle to start the fourth quarter, picking up eight yards. On third and two Dobbs faked to Murray so well that Susan Carol thought the fullback had the ball. But Dobbs suddenly popped up, took two steps back, and lofted a perfect pass to a wide-open G. G. Greene in the end zone.

The stadium was completely silent, except for the five hundred midshipmen who were seated behind the Navy bench.

"Amazing!" Susan Carol yelled as the bench celebrated.

"Not so amazing," Tamara said, pointing at the yellow flag that was lying on the ground only a few yards from where Dobbs had thrown the pass.

The referee turned his mike on to announce the penalty. "Holding, number 70 on the offense. Repeat third down."

He hadn't even turned his mike off before Susan Carol heard Niumatalolo, who was standing way outside the coaching-players area. "Are you kidding me?! On a two-step drop you saw a hold? Were you saving that one for the right time?"

The referee carefully turned his mike off and took a few steps toward Niumatalolo. "Easy, Coach. Don't make it any worse for your players."

That was the wrong thing to say. "Worse for my players?!" Niumatalolo shouted. "You're STEALING THE GAME from my players."

The referee, who had carefully tucked his flag back

into his pocket, took it out again, retreated, and said, "Unsportsmanlike conduct, Navy bench—fifteen yards."

Buddy Green, the defensive coordinator, was now pushing Niumatalolo away from the ref. Two flags had moved Navy from the end zone back to the Notre Dame 35. Navy now had third and twenty-seven.

"They should just try to pick up yardage and get a field goal," Robinson said as Dobbs brought his team back to the line.

Dobbs seemed to be thinking the same way. He faked to Murray, ran to the right, and, as the defense closed, tried to pitch the ball to Greene. Unfortunately, Notre Dame was waiting for the play. Greene was hit just as the ball arrived, it popped loose, and a Notre Dame defensive back picked it up in mid-stride. He was gone—untouched—to the end zone before anyone from Navy realized what had happened.

Just like that, Notre Dame led by a touchdown instead of being down by a touchdown.

"Welcome to South Bend," Tamara said as the stadium erupted in cheers and the fight song—which Susan Carol was now officially getting tired of—blared through the stadium.

"It's all in the timing," Robinson said.

Susan Carol knew he was right. Notre Dame was a great team that didn't need help from the officials. But the right call at the right time could make a huge difference.

Not daunted by the strangely timed penalty and the sudden change in momentum, Navy took the kickoff and began another drive. Notre Dame's defense was tired. It had been on the field for most of the third quarter. The Mids ate up almost seven minutes of clock, running fifteen plays—only one a pass—before Dobbs, again running behind Garrett Smith, punched his way into the end zone with 5:54 left. The extra point tied the game up at 21–21.

The stadium had gone quiet again. It was dark now because the TV time-outs were so long that, even with Navy running the ball, the game had taken more than three hours already. Navy kicked off and Notre Dame picked up two quick first downs, reaching the Navy 37-yard line. The clock ticked down to 3:30.

On first down, Valdiserri faked a handoff and dropped back to pass. But no one from Navy bought the fake. Linebackers Ram Vela and Alan Arnott came in on a blitz from the right side and sacked Valdiserri for an eight-yard loss. Now it was second and eighteen at the Navy 45. Valdiserri dropped back again and saw Arnott blitzing again. He scrambled to his right and tried to throw a pass down the sideline to Bates.

But Navy cornerback Kevin Edwards, who had been lying back behind Bates, jumped in front of him and intercepted the ball. He raced down the sideline with Bates in pursuit. He was finally tackled at the Notre Dame 21-yard line with the clock showing 2:26 to play. Susan Carol realized she was jumping up and down as Edwards sprinted down the sideline. She was surprised when she realized no one on the Navy sideline seemed all that excited.

Then she saw why. The referee was talking to two of

the other officials. He backed away and opened up his microphone. "We have defensive holding on number 15," he said. "That's a five-yard penalty and an automatic first down."

"Oh, wow!" Tamara said. "That's blatant—even here."

Susan Carol heard David Robinson, who was known for never arguing during his years in the NBA, screaming at one of the officials. "Is it written into your contract that you have to make sure Notre Dame wins?"

The official looked over, saw who it was yelling at him, and did a double take. "You need to be quiet, Mr. Robinson," he said, and walked away.

Niumatalolo had thrown his headset to the ground in complete disgust. He was gesturing to the referee to come over and talk to him, but the ref wouldn't even look in his direction. The officials had marked off the penalty and put the ball in play at the Navy 40. The Navy defense, forced to come back on the field, was clearly in shock. Three times Valdiserri handed off and the Irish picked up fourteen yards, moving the ball to the Navy 26. There was under a minute left in the game.

"Looks like they're going to run the clock down and kick a field goal," Tamara said. "That's a little risky."

It became less risky when Valdiserri found Bates for a first down at the 12. Navy used a time-out, no doubt hoping to get the ball back with time on the clock. Notre Dame ran two running plays, and Navy used its last two time-outs. There were thirty-nine seconds left. The Irish ran one more play right to the middle of the field and then let the clock run down to three seconds before calling time out. There was nothing Navy could do.

In came kicker Ted Fusco to try a twenty-five-yarder to win the game.

"Chip shot," Susan Carol said. "I don't think he's missed inside the 40 all year."

Fusco kept his perfect record intact. The ball sailed through the uprights as the clock hit 0:00. Final score: Notre Dame 24–Navy 21. The stadium was going crazy, the fans apparently not caring even a little bit that the game ball should have been presented to the officials. Niumatalolo tried to get to the referee but was stopped by the ever-vigilant security guards. Susan Carol was close enough to hear him say, "I'd like you to look my kids in the eye and explain how you can do this to them!"

Susan Carol felt exactly the same way. The whole game seemed massively unfair. "How *can* they do that?" she said to Tamara.

"Great question," Tamara said. "I doubt anyone will answer it, but it's a great question."

Matt Klunder took Susan Carol into the locker room again. Tamara Mearns had gone to see if she could get in to talk to the officials.

Niumatalolo stood silently in front of his players for a good long while as they settled in around him—some standing, some seated in front of lockers, others taking a knee directly in front of him.

Finally, he took a deep breath, still clearly fighting his emotions. "Look, fellas, we tell you all the time not to worry about the officiating." He paused. "We tell you, and I really believe this, that when all is said and done, games are decided by the players. You get a bad call, then you get a good call. It almost always evens out.

"I can't look you in the eye after this particular game and tell you that's the case. I'd like to, because we're not about making excuses, are we?"

"NO, SIR!" they all shouted back.

"So when the media asks about the holding call that cost us the touchdown, and the hold that cost us the interception, you guys are going to say: 'We don't make excuses at Navy.' That's your answer.

"And the most important thing for all of you to understand is how proud I am of you. You outplayed Notre Dame today, and everyone who watched that game knows it. Right now that isn't much consolation, but try to remember it. There isn't another football team in the country I'd rather be coaching right now.

"One more thing. When they ask you on the hall what happened, you have my permission to say: 'We got screwed.'"

They all got a momentary laugh out of that, and Niumatalolo even forced a smile.

"Okay," he said. "Let's get it in."

They all stood and came together in the middle of the room just as they did at halftime.

Susan Carol whispered to Robinson, "What's 'the hall'?"

"Bancroft Hall," he said. "All four thousand midshipmen live there. It's the largest dormitory on any college campus in the country."

As the players formed their circle, their cry on three was: "Beat Army!"

Susan Carol expected she would hear those words a lot the next few weeks.

THE CADETS

Stevie's experience at West Point for the Army–Georgia Tech game was considerably different. To begin with, there was no snow. And for once he was up earlier than Susan Carol. Kelleher had him walking out the front door of the Thayer by seven o'clock for a tour of the campus. They walked all the way across the Post—going along the Hudson River first, then winding their way up to the Plain and over to Trophy Point, where Kelleher showed Stevie cannons and guns captured in various wars through the years. There were also several more statues.

They stood for a moment at the edge of Trophy Point. They were high up enough to have a great view down the Hudson River. The campus sprawled on one side, and rolling hills went on for miles on the other. The sun had only been up for about an hour and the air was crisp, but the sky was clear. It would be a perfect fall day for football.

"Pretty spectacular, huh?" Kelleher said.

"Unbelievable," Stevie answered, meaning it.

They were back in the hotel by eight for breakfast and out again by nine. Kickoff wasn't until noon, but Kelleher wanted to arrive early to introduce Stevie to various people in the press box.

Before that, though, they stopped at a tailgate party that was held right outside the Holleder Center, where Army's hockey and basketball teams played. Even though he had just eaten, Stevie found the smell of grilling hamburgers irresistible.

"Go ahead," Kelleher said, seeing the look on Stevie's face. "You're still a growing boy."

"I wish I was growing faster," Stevie said.

He was waiting for his hamburger when someone behind him said, "Well, if it isn't my biggest fan."

Stevie recognized the voice instantly but was still surprised to see Duke basketball coach Mike Krzyzewski standing with another legendary basketball coach, Bob Knight, and Pete Dowling, the Secret Service agent.

"Coach K., you remember me?" Stevie said.

Krzyzewski laughed. "Remember you? If it weren't for you and Susan Carol Anderson, I'd have another national championship."

Stevie felt himself turning red. "Well, you know, Coach, we were just trying—"

"To do the right thing," Krzyzewski broke in. "And you did. Wouldn't want it any other way."

"Stevie, I'd like you to meet Bob Knight," Krzyzewski

said, realizing that Stevie was a bit tongue-tied. "And this is Pete Dowling. . . ."

"We met last night," Dowling said.

Knight, who was wearing one of his signature sweaters with an ESPN—his current employer—logo on it, shook hands with Stevie and said, "You're an aspiring sports-writer, I hear."

"Yes, sir."

"So I take it, then, that you're not very bright. Are you going to just stand there all day or are you going to let someone else eat around here?"

Now Stevie was *really* tongue-tied.

"Coach, I thought we had a deal that you wouldn't start beating up on reporters until they're at least twenty-one," Krzyzewski said, making a joke of it. "Stevie, could you ask for three more hamburgers?"

"Um, sure," Stevie said, and signaled for three more to the guy at the grill. "What brings you up here?"

"Girls' field hockey," Knight answered.

Stevie knew that Knight was famous for being brusque, often going out of his way to be rude to reporters. He had risen to fame while winning three national titles and getting into all sorts of trouble at Indiana. He had finished his career at Texas Tech, and Stevie had read that he had become a kinder, gentler curmudgeon since going to work as a commentator on TV. It didn't seem quite that way at the moment.

Krzyzewski forced a laugh. "What Coach meant to say is, the Army Hall of Fame induction dinner is tonight. We both coached at Army early in our careers, and we each have a former player going in. That's why we're here."

"And we hired Agent Dowling for the day to protect us from kids who are media wannabes and budding sycophants," Knight added.

"Well, you don't need protection from me," Stevie shot back. "I'm strictly a newspaper guy, so ESPN is the last place I'd ever work." He was about to congratulate himself for remembering from his eighth-grade vocab class what a sycophant was when he saw the look on Krzyzewski's and Dowling's faces and the definition flew out of his mind. *Oh my God, I just talked back to Bob Knight!*

"You've got some mouth on you, don't you?" Knight said.

Fortunately, the guy grilling the hamburgers intervened at that moment. "Got four fresh ones here," he said, handing them to Stevie, who quickly passed them around.

"I'm sorry—" Stevie started to say.

"That's actually a point," Krzyzewski said. "You *are* in the media now, Coach."

"I need something to drink with my burger," Knight said. "Let's go."

"I'm going to stay here for a minute with Steve," Dowling said. "Coach Knight, it was an honor to meet you. I hope I see you later."

He shook hands with both coaches, who turned into the crowd and were instantly mobbed. Maybe they did need Secret Service protection.

"Pretty gutsy line there, Steve," Dowling said as he picked up his hamburger.

"I can't believe I said that," Stevie said.

"Yeah." Dowling laughed. "He may be seventy, but he's a big guy with a temper."

"No kidding," Stevie said. "What were you doing with them?"

"I met Coach K. years ago when he brought his team to the White House after winning a national title," Dowling said. "He's signed things for charities for me and for my kids. Good guy."

"I know," Stevie said glumly. "My friend Susan Carol *loves* him and everything Duke. I can't stand Duke, but whenever I've met him, he's been really nice."

"Class act," Dowling said. He looked at his watch.

"Are you working?" Stevie asked.

"Soon," Dowling said. "I'm going to meet with the officiating crew when they get here. Some of them will work Army-Navy, so I want to brief them."

"I guess that's a break for you if some of the same guys work both games." Stevie said.

Dowling shook his head. "No, it's not. We requested it. Three officials from this group and four from the Navy–Notre Dame game will call Army-Navy."

"No detail overlooked, huh?" Kelleher said, walking up to join them.

Dowling shrugged. "That's the plan." He glanced at his watch again. "I'm sorry, I've gotta go," he said. "Stevie, keep an eye out for Coach Knight."

Stevie laughed.

Kelleher gave him a look as Dowling walked away. "Did you get yourself into trouble again?" he asked.

"Only a little," Stevie said.

Kelleher shook his head. "Come on, let's get inside the stadium. *Maybe* you'll be safe in there."

Watching the game from the sidelines was thrilling for Stevie. He was amazed by how fast the players moved and by how hard they hit one another. You really didn't see that on TV. Several times when plays came close to where he and Kelleher were standing, he winced at the sound of the contact being made and fully expected the players to remain lying on the ground. And yet they jumped up and ran back to their huddles.

"My mother was right about one thing," he said late in the first quarter. "This is not a game I should play."

He and Kelleher had been joined by two men who knew a lot about football injuries: Tim Kelly, the Army team trainer, and Dean Taylor, a former team doctor who now worked at Duke.

"I'm an Army alum," Taylor said when Kelleher introduced him. "Class of '81. I'm back for the Hall of Fame dinner too."

"He has to keep an eye on Coach K.," Tim Kelly joked. "Anything happens to him and they probably shut Duke down tomorrow."

"True enough," Taylor said.

Taylor had an easy, friendly smile and seemed pretty laid-back—except when calls went against Army.

When a punt hit a Georgia Tech player on the leg and Army fell on it, the packed stadium erupted. But the officials ruled the ball hadn't hit the Tech player and awarded the ball to the Yellow Jackets.

"How in the world can forty thousand people see something and all seven of you miss it completely?" Taylor railed at the side judge, who was standing only a few feet away as Georgia Tech lined up. "What are you looking at, the scenery?"

The side judge shot Taylor a look. Taylor shot him a look right back. At that point Kelly, who watched impassively with his arms folded unless it appeared an Army player might be hurt, put his hand on Taylor's shoulder.

"Easy, Doc," he said.

Kelleher was laughing. "I don't think I've ever heard Dean raise his voice *except* on the sidelines."

Both teams ran almost identical offenses. Paul Johnson, the former Navy coach, was using the same option attack with Georgia Tech that had been so effective at Navy. He'd already won one ACC title with it and was closing in on another one. Army, after getting pounded by Navy's option for years, had hired Rich Ellerson, largely because he ran a similar offense at Cal Poly.

The result was that the defenses knew the offenses well since they practiced against them all the time. When Johnson called for an option pass early in the second quarter from midfield, the Army defense was ready for it and intercepted the pass near the goal line. Every time Army tried to run a toss play for their slotbacks, Georgia Tech was ready for it.

The only score of the first half came late. Army had pinned Georgia Tech near the goal line and forced a punt. The kick was a short one, and Army kick returner Tom Knudson got it to the Tech 37. Army managed to pick up a first down but then stalled at the 21. With forty-two seconds left, field goal kicker Jay Parker hit from thirty-eight yards to make the halftime score Army 3–Georgia Tech 0.

"Not exactly an offensive fireworks display," Kelly said as they crossed the field, heading for the locker room. When they got to the door, Kelly pointed out a middle-aged man in the back of the room.

"Bobby, take Stevie back there to Dicky," he said. "He'll take care of you. I've got to go into the training room and get to work."

Stevie noticed that the coaches had huddled together in an office as soon as everyone piled into the room. Kelleher maneuvered him over to Dicky.

"So, finally, I get to meet a real journalist," Dicky said as he gave Kelleher a hug. "Steve, I'm Dick Hall; it's a pleasure to meet you." He pointed at a table in the corner. "We've got snacks over there; help yourself."

Stevie thanked Hall and scanned the piles of candy, donuts, bagels, and drinks. He had already eaten two hamburgers in addition to breakfast. But he grabbed two packages of spice drops just in case.

"Dicky's been the equipment manager at West Point

since General Thayer founded the place," Kelleher told him.

"Liar," Hall said. "It wasn't until two years later."

Thayer had founded the academy in 1802. And Hall looked to be about fifty.

"Actually, it was 1971," Hall said, cutting Stevie a break. "Right after I got back from Vietnam."

That, Stevie knew, made him older than fifty but younger than Sylvanus Thayer.

The coaches came back into the room and the players broke off into groups. A few minutes later, they all returned to the main locker area and Rich Ellerson came into the room.

"We told you this was going to be a defensive struggle, didn't we?" he said. "This is exactly the game we wanted. It's going to come down to one mistake, one *play*—someone making a play to win the game. Every man in this room is capable of making that play. Each and every one of you. Let's all.be ready when that moment comes, because we don't know when it's going to be."

He paused and looked around the room. "There's no one who has more respect for Coach Johnson than I do. You guys know that. But we owe him a loss, don't we?"

"YES, SIR!" they all answered.

"Let's go."

As soon as the players moved to the middle of the room to huddle up before going back outside, Stevie turned to say something to Dick Hall. But he wasn't there. Stevie looked around the room and found Hall standing by the door. As the players walked through it, Hall gave them each a pat and called each by name, saying, "Let's go, touch the sign." The players all patted Hall back and reached up and touched a sign directly above the door.

As he and Kelleher followed the players out, Stevie paused to read it: NOW I LAY ME DOWN TO BLEED AWHILE BEFORE I RISE AGAIN TO FIGHT.

"What is that?" Stevie asked.

"A lot of college football teams have some sign they post above the locker room door that the players touch for luck or inspiration as they go out," Kelleher said. "Most of them are corny things like 'The team that plays hardest wins the most.'

"This one's a little different. It's an old Army saying from a long-ago battle. Dicky says it was already in place when he got here, so he doesn't know who first posted it. But it means a lot to the players."

Stevie could tell. There was an incredible aura in this place. The history, the tradition—it was a palpable force.

The second half of the game wasn't much different from the first, although the offenses did finally gain some traction. Georgia Tech took the kickoff, finally got its offense in gear, and went eighty yards, culminating the drive when their huge fullback bulled into the end zone from four yards out.

"They took almost eight minutes off the clock," Tim Kelly said as the extra point made it 7–3. "Our offense needs to give the defense some rest right now."

It did. Trent Steelman, the Army quarterback, wasn't

all that big, but he began finding some room after a couple of good runs up the middle by fullback Tom Nottingham. Then he faked a run, dropped back, and found tight end Michael Arnott open for a twenty-two-yard pickup to the Georgia Tech 23. But the drive stalled there and Parker had to come in and try another field goal, this one from thirty-six yards out.

The kick began hooking left as it got near the goal line, causing everyone on the sidelines to lean to the right, trying to guide the ball through. Which kind of worked—the ball hit the left upright and ricocheted through the goalpost.

"Thank God," Taylor said.

"I'm not sure he was involved," Kelly said. "But we'll take it."

There was a little more than a minute left in the third quarter, and Georgia Tech led 7–6.

Stevie noticed that the wind had picked up and the temperature had dropped since kickoff, but the game was going quickly—it wasn't even three o'clock. As the third quarter ended, the band played the Army fight song and the four thousand cadets—all of them standing—went crazy, singing so loudly that "On, brave old army team, on to the fra-aaay" echoed in Stevie's ears.

If a team could win on heart, Army had the game locked up.

OVERTIME

Early in the fourth quarter, with the Yellow Jackets facing third and two on their own 37, Georgia Tech coach Paul Johnson made a bold call.

Thinking Army would be looking for a run made sense, since Tech had only thrown six passes at that point. So Johnson called for a quick pass on a sideline route, figuring he'd at least get a first down and might pick up big yardage. But Army cornerback Mario Hill didn't fall for the fake, and when the Tech quarterback threw the ball, Hill stepped in front of the intended receiver, intercepted the ball, and had nothing but open field in front of him as he raced to the end zone.

The Army sideline exploded, and Stevie noticed that even Tim Kelly unfolded his arms long enough to hug both Dean Taylor and Dick Hall. Stevie wondered if this was the one big play Coach Ellerson had talked about at halftime.

Army went for a two-point conversion to try to make the lead 14–7. Quarterback Trent Steelman took it himself—and drove right into the end zone. The band played the fight song again. The place was jumping.

But Georgia Tech hadn't run up a 9–1 record without having dealt with some tough situations. The Yellow Jackets calmly pieced together a drive that took another seven minutes off the clock and tied the score at 14 with just under four minutes left in the game. Each team got the ball once more; neither came close to scoring.

So the game went to overtime.

In the NFL, overtime was played like a real game: there was a coin toss, followed by a kickoff, and the first team to score won the game.

But in college football, it was completely different. A coin toss decided who got possession first. Then the ball was placed on the 25-yard line and the team tried to score from there. Regardless of whether they scored or not, the other team also got the ball at the 25. So if the first team to have the ball scored a touchdown, the other team had to match that or the game was over. If the first team kicked a field goal, then the other team could tie with a field goal or win the game with a touchdown. If the score was still tied after each team had the ball, the game continued with another pair of possessions.

Georgia Tech won the toss and elected to defend first.

"You always want to let the other team have the ball first so you know exactly what you need to do when *you* get the ball," Kelleher said.

"But if they go to a second overtime, Georgia Tech gets the ball first, right?" Stevie said.

Kelleher nodded. "Yeah, they alternate," he said. "Plus, Army gets to decide which end of the field they're going to play on, and they're going to make Tech play right in front of the corps."

It was clear to Stevie, from Army's play-calling, that Coach Ellerson still believed in his defense: a fullback dive got two yards, a quarterback sprint gained two more, and another fullback dive was good for three. So it was fourth down, with the ball on the 18-yard line, and Jay Parker and the field goal team trotted on.

"Ellerson's taking no chances," Kelleher said. "I'm not sure that's a good play."

"I don't like it at all," Taylor said. "They've already driven the length of the field on us twice in this half. Now they only have to go twenty-five yards to win the game."

Parker nailed the field goal from thirty-five yards and Army led 17–14.

There was no break with change of possession; Georgia Tech's offense trotted out, as did the Army defense.

Johnson had a reputation as a bit of a riverboat gambler in his play-calling. And even though a bold call had resulted in an interception earlier in the game, he was still thinking big. On first down, he called for a play-action fake to the fullback, and then Tech quarterback Lamar

Goodes rolled out right and connected with a receiver streaking toward the sideline. He caught the ball in full stride at the 10 and looked like he might score, until one of Army's safeties, Derek Klein, fought off a block and pushed him out of bounds on the 7-yard line.

"I just knew it." Taylor shook his head.

"They haven't scored yet, Doc," Dicky Hall said.

"First and goal on the seven . . . ," Taylor said.

Johnson went for the quick kill on the next play, calling another play-action pass, but this time Army had everyone covered and Goodes threw the ball away. Second and goal. On second down, Tech went with a run up the middle and plowed to the 4-yard line. Instinctively, Stevie looked up at the clock and then realized it was at 0:00. There was no clock in overtime.

"What's he do here?" Tim Kelly asked.

"He might call the same play, try to fool us," Hall said.

"Roll out," Taylor said. "Let the quarterback make a play with his feet or his arm depending on what he sees."

Taylor had it right. Goodes rolled out, his arm cocked as if to pass. At the last possible moment, he pulled the ball down and charged toward the corner of the end zone. Two Army defenders came up to stop him, and they wrestled him down very close to the goal line.

For a split second, it looked as if Goodes might have scored. There was no signal from the officials. Finally the referee stood up with his right arm raised above his head in a clenched fist—the signal for fourth down. Nearly everyone in the stadium breathed a sigh of relief.

Stevie could see Paul Johnson at least five yards out onto the field pointing in the direction of the press box.

"He wants them to review it," Kelleher said. "He thinks they scored."

"You can't blame him for asking, right?" Stevie said. From where he was standing, it was impossible to know if Goodes had gotten over the goal line or not.

"Yes, they really should review in this situation," Kelleher said. "This is one time where you want to be a hundred percent sure."

"The play is under review," the referee said, turning on his microphone. "The ruling on the field is fourth down."

And so they waited. Two minutes went by, then three. The crowd grew restless.

"The rule should really be that if they can't be sure after two minutes of review, then the call on the field stands," Kelleher said. "This is ridiculous."

Another minute passed. Finally, the referee took off the headset that connected him to the press box and trotted back onto the field.

"After further review, the ruling on the field stands. . . ."

He continued to talk, but Stevie couldn't hear him over the wild cheering coming from the corps, which was directly behind where they were standing.

"Now what does Johnson do?" Stevie asked.

"Any other coach, I'd say he kicks the field goal and plays on in a second overtime," Kelleher said. "But that's not usually Paul's way. He always thinks he can come up with a play to get what he needs, and it looks like he only needs about a foot."

Johnson had called time out to think about it, and both teams were huddling around their coaches. The Army players were so close to Stevie, he could hear Rich Ellerson's voice even over the din coming from the corps.

"He's going to go for it," Ellerson said. "He thinks they can make a play and win the game. So this is where *we* make a play and win the game. They will *not* run up the middle—that's not what he does in these situations. We're going to sell out on the quarterback sprint, okay? If he goes the other way, then I lost the game, so don't even worry about it. Ignore the middle—we want maximum coverage on the sides."

The teams trotted back out. Tech huddled up, even though the play had clearly been called on the sideline. Goodes brought his team to the line, barked signals, and took the snap. At first, Stevie thought Ellerson had blown it, because Goodes appeared to put the ball into his fullback's stomach and the fullback flew through the air into the end zone.

But the fullback didn't have the ball. Goodes had pulled it away at the last minute and was sprinting to his left, to the near corner, only a few yards from where Stevie, Kelleher, Hall, Kelly, and Taylor were standing. As Goodes tried to turn his shoulder toward the goal line, Stevie realized that at least a half dozen black-shirted defenders were pursuing him.

He held his breath as Goodes got to about the 3-yard

line and tried to dive at the corner of the end zone. But at least three Army defenders were right in front of him. He struggled forward for an instant and then collapsed under a pile of black shirts, still a yard from the goal line.

Stevie heard a cannon go off somewhere and saw Kelly, Taylor, and Hall jump into a three-man hug. The entire Army team left the bench to celebrate. Stevie noticed something else: the Army defenders who had tackled Goodes had not gone into celebration mode right away. Instead, they reached down and helped him to his feet. Handshakes and hugs were exchanged.

Kelleher had a huge smile on his face. "You understand," he yelled over the screams and shouts cascading down on them, "that there is NO way this team should beat a team with Georgia Tech's talent. These kids do this stuff on guts and heart."

As Kelleher talked, Stevie saw the Army players, having celebrated and then shaken the hands of the Georgia Tech players, walking back in their direction. The Tech players, he noticed, were right behind them.

"What's this?" he asked.

"Just watch," Kelleher said.

The Army players lined up in neat rows, facing the corps of cadets. The Tech players stood directly behind them.

"Ladies and gentlemen, please rise for the playing of the Army alma mater," the public address announcer said.

Stevie noticed the Army players come to attention, as

did the entire corps. After the song everyone yelled, "Beat Navy!"

Kelleher explained. "Army, Navy, and Air Force all play their alma maters after each game. When they play each other, the losing team goes first, then they cross the field and do it for the winning team. You see guys who have been trying to kill one another for three hours crying on each other's shoulders.

"Paul Johnson was at Navy, so he understands the tradition. That's why his guys stayed. It doesn't always happen that way."

"Cool," Stevie said.

Hall was right behind them. "Come on, hustle up," he said. "You don't want to miss the song."

"The song?" Stevie said. "They just played the song."

Hall shook his head. "That was the alma mater. After we win, the players sing the song. You really need to hear it."

Hall wasn't kidding. As soon as the players had piled into the locker room, still hugging one another joyously, Ellerson jumped on a chair and called for silence, which he got very quickly.

"I don't need to tell *you* what a great win that was," he said. "I'm not sure there's a game in which you earned the right to sing the song more than this one. So, let's do it!"

With that, the entire team began singing the Army fight song, belting it out in a way that even Stevie recognized was way off-key, but it didn't matter. Stevie had been in winning locker rooms after the World Series, the Super Bowl, and the Final Four. And he'd never seen a group of athletes happier than the Army players.

He and Kelleher lingered for a while. Hall introduced them to Ellerson just before the coach left for his postgame press conference.

"That was a great call on the last play," Stevie said as they shook hands.

Ellerson waved him off. "Against that offense they can *tell* you what they're going to do and it's still hard to stop," he said. "The kids just made a great play."

Stevie liked him right away. So many coaches loved taking bows after wins. Clearly, Ellerson wasn't like that.

Hall also took Stevie around the room so he could meet some of the players, explaining to them that Stevie was going to be around a fair bit in the next couple of weeks prior to the Navy game.

"I know who you are," Mario Hill said. "I read all about you and your partner, Susan Carol, right? In my newspaper back home."

"Where are you from?" Stevie asked, then felt embarrassed because he could easily have checked it in the media guide.

"Goldsboro, North Carolina," Hill said.

Stevie nodded. Susan Carol's hometown.

"I hope I get to meet Susan Carol too," Hill said. "You two are quite a team."

* * *

They were on their way back up to the press box so Kelleher could write his column for the Sunday paper when Stevie heard from the other half of the team.

He checked his phone and discovered a text from Susan Carol: *Halftime. Great game. FREEZING to death. Miss you.*

When they reached the press box, Stevie found a TV that was showing the end of the Navy–Notre Dame game. Just looking at the snow and the bundled-up fans in the stands made him feel cold.

Watching your game now, he texted Susan Carol back. *Army's win amazing.* He paused for a second and then added: *Miss you too. Not the same.* They really were a good team.

Stevie heard a roar from the TV after Navy intercepted a pass only to have the officials give the ball back to Notre Dame because of a holding call.

"I don't see it," NBC analyst Pat Haden said. "If there was a hold, the official must have had an angle we don't have."

"It's that kind of call along with the hold that denied Navy a touchdown earlier that makes people occasionally wonder if the Irish don't get the benefit of the doubt from the officials in this stadium," Tom Hammond added.

Stevie was surprised to hear Haden and Hammond say that. He had watched enough Notre Dame games to know that Hammond and Haden almost always sang the praises of the Irish. It had to have been a truly awful call if they were criticizing the officials, even mildly.

Kelleher walked up behind him, computer slung over his shoulder, as the game was winding down.

"Irish are going to pull it out here, huh?" he said as Notre Dame was lining up for a field goal to win the game.

When Stevie told him about the holding call, Kelleher shook his head. "I wish I was surprised."

The field goal split the uprights and the Notre Dame players celebrated. Stevie looked for Susan Carol on the sidelines but didn't see her.

He heard her loud and clear, though, when she called later to tell him about the game. Once she'd had a chance to review parts of the game on TV and see it from all angles, she'd only gotten madder than she'd been on the field.

"Let 'em have it," Stevie told her.

And in her story for Monday's *Post* labeled "News Analysis," she did.

> There are some who say the luck of the Irish has very little to do with luck, especially in Notre Dame Stadium. That was never more evident than Saturday, when two controversial holding calls from the officials were the difference between a Notre Dame win and a Navy win.
>
> In the fourth quarter, with the game tied at 14 all, quarterback Ricky Dobbs lofted a perfect touchdown pass to G. G. Greene. But

the play was called back on an offensive holding call. Navy's coach, Ken Niumatalolo, was enraged by the call. But holding is not a reviewable play, so he was left to vent his frustration at referee Mike Daniels, saying, "You're stealing the game from my players!" Daniels tacked on a charge of unsportsmanlike conduct for the Navy bench.

On the very next play, Notre Dame was able to capitalize on this second chance— picking up a fumbled pitch and running it back for a touchdown to put them ahead.

Navy battled back against a tired Notre Dame defense and put together a fifteen-play drive to tie the game again with just under six minutes left.

Notre Dame seemed poised to answer back when Navy cornerback Kevin Edwards jumped the route and intercepted a Roger Valdiserri pass, returning it to the Notre Dame 21. But again, a holding call reversed a Navy big play and gave the ball back to Notre Dame, along with a first down.

With only three seconds on the clock, Notre Dame was able to kick a field goal and win the game 24–21.

NBA Hall of Famer and Navy grad David Robinson was on the sidelines making his opinions known, wondering aloud if it was in the officiating contract that Notre Dame had to win at home.

NBC analysts with multiple replay angles could find no evidence of holding in either instance, prompting Tom Hammond to comment, "It's that kind of call . . . that makes people occasionally wonder if the Irish don't get the benefit of the doubt from the officials in this stadium."

When a reporter visited the officials' locker room after the game, referee Mike Daniels was belligerent. "We have no obligation to talk to the media," Daniels said. "We all get pretty sick and tired of people blaming us for everything that goes wrong. Go find another scapegoat."

While it's true that officials are often cast as the villains and rarely the heroes of a game, the pattern of controversial calls in Notre Dame Stadium has many asking for further inquiry. Bad calls will always be a part of the game—officials are only human. But when a game is decided by the officials and not the players, the coaches and players deserve a thorough review and a thoughtful response. There have been long-standing questions about how officiating is run in college football, and games like this only add fuel to the fire of suspicion that referees have an incentive to slant calls in favor of the conference that pays their salaries—or, in this case, the team with its own TV network.

Honest mistakes can be forgiven if they are followed by honest apologies. But since the officials in this case were so clearly unwilling to review their own performance, they will have to live with the accusations of those who have reviewed it—and found it not only wanting, but suspect.

GAME DAY: 1 HOUR, 36 MINUTES TO KICKOFF

With the march-ons complete and the cadets now in their seats engaging in good-natured razzing with the midshipmen, the teams began coming onto the field to warm up.

Stevie noticed they didn't come out all at once. The kickers came out first, apparently so they could boom kicks all over the field without getting in anybody's way. Then the rest of the players came out by position: linebackers, defensive backs, linemen. The so-called skill position players—quarterbacks, running backs, and receivers—came last.

Stevie and Susan Carol both saw players they'd gotten to know well, but there was no time for chat—the players were all focused on getting warmed up for their biggest game of the year.

By eleven o'clock, the field was filled with players and

the stands also appeared full. Stevie had no doubt there were still some people trying to get through security, but it looked to him as if most people had heeded all the warnings about arriving early.

Susan Carol saw that the officials were also on the field, warming up. She hadn't realized when she wrote her story about the officials at Notre Dame that some of them would be working this game as well. She tried to unobtrusively keep Stevie between her and Mike Daniels, and for the first time she found herself wishing that Stevie was taller.

She was glad when Kelleher, Pete Dowling, and Bob Campbell returned after another pregame check—they offered more cover.

"Another hour and we'll have the president in his seat and be seventy-five percent of the way home," Dowling said.

"Seventy-five percent?" Susan Carol asked.

"The president has to cross the field at halftime," Dowling said. "That's another high-alert moment for us. And then we have to get him home."

"And still no sign of trouble?" Stevie asked.

"None. The people we've been watching are still outside tailgating. Haven't even made a move to come inside."

Campbell said, "We had their license plates and knew what parking lot they had a pass for, so their cars were checked thoroughly coming in."

"And you didn't find anything?" Susan Carol said.

"Nothing but beer and cameras and extra scarves," Dowling said.

Susan Carol gave them credit for that. She wished she had an extra scarf about now. Even wearing long underwear, a down coat, a hat, gloves, and a scarf, she was still cold. But the sun was warming things up—it might hit forty by noon.

The PA announcer was telling everyone that the players would be clearing the field by 11:20 so the parachutists could make their jumps into the stadium.

"Marine One doesn't leave the White House until that's over," Dowling explained. "Once the president leaves the ground, the airspace around here is completely locked down until he's back inside the White House after the game."

"What about planes heading to National; isn't this right along their route?" Kelleher asked.

"Sometimes it is, depending on the wind," Dowling said. "But from eleven fifteen until about four o'clock, they can't use this flight path. Fortunately, it's a good-weather day, so they've got lots of options. Shouldn't cause any delays."

Stevie had a game-day itinerary that was planned right to the minute. The parachutists were supposed to begin landing at 11:26.

And sure enough, when the players had all gone back to their locker rooms, he heard the sound of a plane overhead.

Ninety thousand faces turned up to the sky to watch as

eight specks started falling. Then one by one, eight enormous parachutes unfurled. In the sky they seemed to be gliding slowly and smoothly, but the closer they came to the ground, the more Stevie could see they were moving at an incredible speed. Skydiving—yet another thing he wasn't eager to try.

The divers left ribbons of red and blue smoke streaming behind them. They must have had some kind of special equipment in their shoes. It was a great effect.

The PA announcer told the divers' names as they touched down on the field and worked to gather in their still-billowing chutes. Amazingly, the last diver, who was carrying the official game ball, touched down right on the huge Army-Navy game medallion painted at midfield. The referee met him there to accept the ball to great applause.

To Stevie's surprise, he also heard a smattering of boos. But then he saw they were coming from the Navy side—clearly some people had recognized the referee.

Pete Dowling had one hand on his earpiece. "Marine One is in the air," he reported. "We'll have wheels down here at eleven thirty-eight."

"Everything is on schedule, then," Susan Carol said.

"So far," Dowling said. "We all just want to see a good football game and have that be the story of the day."

That sounded good to Susan Carol. And just about perfect to Stevie. He hadn't really fully appreciated how hard the Secret Service's job was until a small incident had set off fireworks at the Army-Navy lunch.

THE ARMY-NAVY LUNCH

Stevie walked into Lincoln Financial Field on a blustery Tuesday afternoon. The mild weather from the weekend was long gone, replaced by the kind of windy, cold day you would expect in Philadelphia two days before Thanksgiving.

Kelleher had left his name on the list at the door and, for once, no one asked him what a fourteen-year-old was doing on a media list. The way Kelleher had described the traditional Army-Navy lunch made it sound a lot like a press conference—in other words, boring. On the plus side, it was lunch—which made the assignment a lot more palatable to Stevie.

He was surprised by how much security there was when he walked inside. There were two men—clearly Secret Service—posted at the door to the lobby. They asked him why he was there, and when he said, "The Army-Navy lunch," they nodded and let him inside. Even though no one questioned his presence on the list, he had to show ID, get a pass, and then go through a metal detector before he could proceed to the elevators.

Worried he was now late, Stevie waited impatiently for the elevator. But then coach Ken Niumatalolo, accompanied by two young men in snappy blue uniforms and another man in a suit, joined him.

"Coach Niumatalolo, my name is Steve Thomas," he said, putting out a hand. "I think you met my friend Susan Carol Anderson at Notre Dame."

Niumatalolo smiled. "Yes! Susan Carol's become very popular on the Yard. The team really appreciated her story on the officials—she could say a lot of things we couldn't." He turned to the two guys in uniform. "Steve, these are our captains, Ricky Dobbs and Wyatt Middleton. And this is Scott Strasemeier, our sports information director."

Stevie shook hands all around. He was familiar with Dobbs, who had been mentioned as a Heisman Trophy candidate during the season.

"Thank her for us, will you?" Dobbs said.

"She'll be glad to know you liked it."

"Is Susan Carol really just a freshman in high school?" Middleton asked.

Stevie nodded. "People think she's older all the time," he said. "It's because she's so tall."

When the elevator finally arrived and they all filed in, Stevie said, "So, was there enough security for you out there?"

"They told us Vice President Biden may be coming," Niumatalolo said. "If you think this is bad, wait until the game when he *and* the president are both there."

Stevie knew he wasn't kidding.

There were people waiting once they got off the elevators to whisk the Navy guys inside. Stevie had to stop again so the Secret Service could check the name on his credential against their list. Once he had passed that test, he went into a large dining room that was set up with a podium up front and a buffet—as yet untouched—in the back. Pete Dowling was standing off to the side with another agent.

Dowling waved him over when he saw him. "Steve, I want you to meet my partner, Bob Campbell."

Stevie knew the name right away. "My friend Susan Carol was impressed with the way you handled Coach Kelly's over-vigilant security guard at Notre Dame."

Campbell shook his head. "I wish Susan Carol hadn't seen that," he said. "I didn't want to make a big deal of it, but in our business there's nothing worse than dealing with amateurs."

Dowling laughed. "We've got a lot of that ahead the next couple weeks," he said.

"What do you mean?" Stevie asked.

"We need so many people that we bring in guys from out-of-town police departments," Dowling said. "Not that they're amateurs. I was a cop once. But we try to keep them on the routine stuff, like checking people through security."

"What about today?" Stevie asked. "Is all of this because Biden's coming?"

Dowling shot him a look. "How'd you know that?"

"I rode the elevator with Coach Niumatalolo," Stevie said.

Dowling shook his head. "You *are* a good reporter. Two minutes in an elevator and you already know more about what's happening than I'd like. Yes, this is all for the vice president."

"Anything happen so far that makes you nervous?" Stevie asked.

Dowling smiled. "Nothing I'd mention."

Fair enough, Stevie thought. He'd try a different tack. "Has there *ever* been a problem at an Army-Navy game in the past?"

He was surprised when Dowling laughed. "Not really a problem," he said. "But someone you know almost didn't get into the game a couple years ago because he was considered a security risk."

"Who?" Stevie asked.

"Well, to use the name that came up on his FBI file, Robert Wilson Kelleher," Dowling said.

"Bobby?" Stevie was shocked. "A security risk?"

Dowling shrugged. "He had written a column saying President Bush had no business coming to the Army-Navy game since he had already put players who had graduated from both schools in harm's way in Iraq and was continuing to do so even though the war was a debacle. The column raised some eyebrows."

"So what happened?"

"I intervened. I told them I'd known Bobby for years and that being a liberal didn't make him a threat. Even so, they combed through his past pretty carefully before they cleared him."

"Wow," Stevie said, reverting to his favorite word.

Stevie saw his pal Dick Jerardi approaching.

"Didn't think I'd see you here, Stevie," Jerardi said. "No school today?"

Stevie explained that it was a half day before the Thanksgiving holiday and introduced Jerardi to Dowling and Campbell.

Jerardi shook hands with both men. "Lotta security for lunch—all for Biden?"

Dowling groaned. "Does *everyone* know about Biden coming?"

"One of the Philly cops I know told me," Jerardi said.

"Everyone likes to run their mouth," Dowling said.

Stevie saw several people putting hot food out on the buffet. That was good news. "When do we eat?" he asked Jerardi.

"As soon as the mayor, the governor, and the vice president get here," Jerardi said.

"The mayor and the governor are coming too?" Stevie said, surprised.

"Yup," Jerardi said. "Governor Rendell played a big role in making sure the game stayed in Philadelphia most of the time when he was mayor. And Mayor Nutter wants to be sure everyone remembers the game is back here the next three years. Plus, you think either one is going to pass up a chance for a photo op with the VP?"

Dowling was about to say something, but his cell phone started to chirp.

"What's up, Mike?" he said, putting his phone to his left ear. He had a wire of some kind, Stevie noticed, in his right ear.

As he listened, his smile disappeared. "Got it," he said. He snapped the phone shut and then, just like Stevie had seen in the movies and on TV, he put his arm up to his mouth and started talking into his wrist.

"Crash the stadium," he said very quietly. "Two non-cleareds through the gate, location unknown."

He pushed Campbell in the direction of the door. "Get the elevators shut down, Bob," he said. He began waving his arms to get people's attention.

"Ladies and gentlemen, ladies and gentlemen, *please*, I need your attention right now."

The room quieted quickly. "My name is Special Agent Peter Dowling. I'm with the Secret Service, and we have a situation. There's a possibility that this is a false alarm, and I do not believe that you are in danger. But for now, I need everyone to stay in this room and to *please* turn off your cell phones. I'm sure we'll have this resolved shortly, but I'm asking you to bear with us for a few moments."

"What's going on?" Stevie asked.

Dowling seemed focused on making sure cell phones

got turned off. "I can't give you details," he said. "In fact, I don't have many details. But two guys came into the building who raised suspicions."

"How?" Stevie asked.

Dowling looked around for a second as if making sure no one else was listening. *"Off the record,"* he said. "They checked in under the names Michael Barkann and Brian Schiff."

"From Comcast SportsNet," Stevie said. "I know them both."

"So do I," Dowling said. "But the people in the lobby didn't. They just checked their names off and must not have looked very closely at their IDs and their faces. That's what I was just talking about with amateurs— they're either obnoxiously careful or too lax. The two guys cleared the metal detectors, but then they didn't get on the elevator to come up here."

"How do you know that?"

"There's a surveillance camera in the elevator waiting area. They walked past the elevators and into the stadium."

Stevie felt a slight chill go through him.

Dowling held up his hand as Stevie started to ask another question. Then he talked into his wrist again. "Mike, hold them in the limos. If we don't resolve this in five minutes, I want them out of here."

"Who?" Stevie asked.

"The mayor and the governor," Dowling said. "We're holding them outside. The VP is five minutes out. If we don't find these guys before he gets here, we're going to turn him around."

"That might be tough in a stadium this big," Stevie said.

"Exactly," Dowling said. "I have to get going."

Stevie noticed that police officers had appeared at all the exits.

"Oh, Steve, one more thing," Dowling said. "I need you to turn off your cell phone."

Stevie had forgotten. He took it out of his pocket. "How come you need the cell phones off?" he asked.

"To make sure the intruders don't have a contact in this room," Dowling said.

Stevie looked down to turn off his phone. When he looked back up, Dowling was gone.

PRANKSTERS?

The next hour was both tense and intense.

Not long after Dowling had left, another agent appeared, introducing himself as the head of the Secret Service's Philadelphia field office. He assured everyone that the area was "locked down temporarily" only as a precaution and that everything would be back to normal shortly. A few minutes later he returned to say that the lockdown would continue for a few more minutes, but people were welcome to go through the buffet line.

"Can we go to the bathroom?" someone shouted.

"Not just yet," the agent said. "Soon. I promise."

But it wasn't soon. Stevie was seated at a table with Jerardi, Dei Lynam from Comcast SportsNet, and Derek Klein, one of the Army team captains, all of them wondering what could be going on.

Stevie had told the table what Dowling had said. "Michael was never coming today," Lynam said. "I don't think Shifty was either. I'd like to know if someone from the station put their names on the list. . . ."

"Or if someone who knew they wouldn't be here did," Jerardi put in.

"Problem is, we can't call anyone right now to find out," Lynam said.

Stevie could tell the room was getting restless. He needed to go to the bathroom too. Normally he would have welcomed an hour with Derek Klein, but he was too distracted to really focus on any kind of interview. But he did get some background. Klein was a Michigan kid, a coach's son who had come to Army as a quarterback but had been converted to safety after his sophomore year.

"Trent Steelman was better than I was at quarterback," he said. "And I wanted to play. So I went to the coaches before spring practice two years ago and asked if I could move. At first they said no, they needed me as a backup QB because I had experience. I told them I didn't want to graduate without having made a serious contribution. This was the only way I thought I'd get a chance to do it."

One thing Stevie had noticed in his brief exposure to the Army and Navy athletes was that they almost never used the phrase "you know." And they looked you right in the eye when they spoke to you. When he had met Niumatalolo with his captains downstairs, they both repeated his name when they shook his hand: "Steve, nice to meet you." Stevie had grown accustomed to athletes who didn't even bother to take their headphones off when being introduced.

Klein was about to tell a story about an old teammate who was now serving in Iraq when Stevie saw Pete Dowling walk back into the room.

"Ladies and gentlemen, we're all clear," he said. "I apologize for the inconvenience. We thought we had an intruder, but it turned out to be a miscommunication. I'm told Mr. Needle will start the program in a few minutes."

Stevie knew, because he'd seen his name in the paper and his face on TV, that Larry Needle was the head of the Philadelphia Sports Congress, a group that tried to bring events like Army-Navy to Philadelphia. Needle had now moved to the microphone at the front of the room. "Folks, I'm really sorry about all this; I know we all are. Unfortunately, because of the mix-up, the mayor had to head back to his office. Governor Rendell, I'm told, is on his way up right now and—"

"I'm here right now, Larry," a voice said from the back of the room.

Stevie looked around and saw Ed Rendell—with lots of security in tow—walking through the tables to the podium. Stevie knew that Rendell was not a politician who pretended to like sports because it played well with the voters. In fact, he was such an ardent Eagles fan that during his days as mayor, he appeared weekly on an Eagles postgame show on Comcast.

Rendell strode to the microphone and Needle moved away to give him room.

"I apologize for all the hoo-ha these last few minutes," Rendell said. "We were hoping to surprise everyone by having Vice President Biden join us today. But with the mix-up, the Secret Service turned the VP around. Better safe than sorry. He sends his regrets; he really did want to be here.

"And Mayor Nutter also sends his apologies for not being able to stay. He had a meeting at city hall he had to get back to. I think he would have said the same thing I'm going to say if he had been able to stay: 'Philadelphia *is* the home of the Army-Navy game.' We don't mind loaning it out for a year every now and then, but I think everyone agrees this is where the game belongs. We love having everyone from both schools in town, and I think Larry and his guys have done a great job in making all of you feel welcome.

"So, I hope you have a great game this year down in, what is it—Landover, Maryland? That's another thing I'm proud of—Philadelphia's stadiums and arenas are *in* Philadelphia, not in the suburbs. But I hope you have a great game. I plan to be there with the president and the vice president, so I look forward to seeing all of you there and then back *here*, where you belong, a year from now."

There was enthusiastic applause as he finished.

"Governor," Needle said, stepping back to the microphone, "do you mind taking a few questions from the media while you're here?"

"Glad to," Rendell said.

There were a couple of questions about Philadelphia's commitment to keeping the game in future years. Then Jerardi stood up.

"Hey, Dick, long time, no see," Rendell said.

"Thanks, Governor, we miss you on the postgame show," Jerardi said. "Since the incident is now over, can you give us some idea about what happened earlier?"

Rendell appeared to be ready for the question. He nodded at Jerardi.

"Sure, Dick," he said. "Two people got into the stadium who shouldn't have. The Secret Service was understandably alarmed. But it turned out to be just a couple of kids from Penn on a fraternity initiation assignment."

"Fraternity initiation?"

Rendell nodded. "Apparently they were supposed to get their picture taken with me—you know, the old Penn grad who is now governor. They had no idea there'd be extra security because of the vice president or that the vice president was even coming.

"They were actually pretty clever. They called Comcast, claiming to be from Larry's office, and asked who was coming to the lunch. Then they called Larry's office, claiming to be from Comcast, and added two names to the list of attendees.

"That got them through the door, and I guess no one looked closely enough at their IDs. That's where the breakdown was. So they went into the concourse to wait for me to come in, hoping they could get a picture."

"So what took so long to sort things out, then?" Jerardi asked, which was what Stevie had been thinking.

Rendell nodded again. "When the folks downstairs realized they hadn't gotten on the elevators but were somewhere else in the stadium, they called up here, and the Secret Service shut the place down. By then there were police and Secret Service all over, and the kids panicked and hid. Took a while to find them."

"Were they arrested?" Jerardi asked.

"No," Rendell said. "Their stories checked. They weren't carrying anything resembling a weapon—except their cell phone cameras. They were given a stern lecture and sent back to Penn."

"Last question," Jerardi said. "Did they get their picture?"

Rendell shook his head. "Secret Service wouldn't let them anywhere near me. Not because they were dangerous, but because they caused everyone so much trouble. When I say they got a stern lecture, I mean they got a *stern* lecture.

"Dick, they're telling me I'm out of time; we need to get the coaches and players up here. Let's get back to the reason we're all really here!"

With that, Rendell escaped, giving Needle the microphone so he could begin his introductions of the coaches and players.

Jerardi sat down and leaned over to Stevie. "You buy that story?" he asked.

Stevie looked at him. "You don't?"

"Maybe," Jerardi said. "But if I had a relationship with Agent Dowling like you seem to have, I'd find him and see what he has to say. Rendell had almost too many details. He sounded very well coached to me."

"He's a politician," Stevie said.

"Good point," Jerardi said. "They're very coachable."

As soon as the lunch was over, Stevie tried to find Dowling and Campbell. The police were no help, claiming they had no idea who Stevie was even talking about. Stevie finally found the guy who had introduced himself to the crowd as the head of the Philadelphia field office.

"Bud Keyser," he said, shaking hands when Stevie introduced himself. "I know who you are; Pete told me that you were shadowing him on some Army-Navy stuff."

"Do you know where he is right now?" Stevie asked.

"Yeah, I do," Keyser said. "He's on his way back to Washington. Once everything was clear, he took off."

Stevie wondered what he should do next. He looked around and saw Niumatalolo finishing up a one-on-one with a local TV station and waving at Larry Needle.

He thanked Keyser and made his way in that direction.

"Interesting day," he heard Niumatalolo say to Needle. "Sort of more than we bargained for."

"No kidding," Needle said. "Who'd have thought two kids from a fraternity could hold us all hostage for an hour?"

They shook hands and Niumatalolo turned and saw Stevie.

"Hey, Steve," he said. "You got a little more of a story than coaches and players talking about how much they're looking forward to the game, didn't you?"

Stevie nodded. "That's for sure. Did you happen to see Mr. Dowling once everything was all clear?"

"The Secret Service agent? Yeah. Coach Ellerson and I spoke to him earlier. He explained that they had turned the vice president around just to be safe."

"How'd he seem? Concerned or annoyed?"

Niumatalolo shot him a look, then smiled. "Always reporting, huh? He was calm and professional. Off the record, though, I thought he seemed kind of ticked off. He said something about having enough to worry about without panicking people over a fraternity prank."

"Thanks, Coach, I appreciate it."

"No problem—I hope we'll be seeing you and Susan Carol on the Yard after Thanksgiving."

"We'll be there."

Niumatalolo went off to round up his players. Stevie could see why Susan Carol had liked him so much—he was very friendly and talkative, probably much to Dowling's chagrin. Then Stevie was struck by a scary thought. Dowling might have *wanted* Niumatalolo to pass on the fraternity prank story, along with Rendell. Maybe Dowling was ticked off because the story *wasn't* that simple.

* * *

Kelleher must have said "Are you kidding me?" a dozen times as Stevie filled him in over the phone on his way home. "Nothing ever happens at that lunch!"

"So maybe it *was* just a fraternity prank," said Stevie.

"I know Pete Dowling and Bob Campbell pretty well. They're careful, but they don't panic. They must have been really nervous about something to turn Biden around.

"And Jerardi's right—Rendell was most likely briefed beforehand so he could be the face of the story. Secret Service doesn't like to put itself out front on anything unless there's no choice."

"So should I call Dowling? Should you?" Stevie asked.

"Right now, neither of us should call," Kelleher said. "If something is going on, he'll be too spooked to talk. I'd let it simmer a few days, and maybe when you see Dowling again in person, you can get an explanation that makes more sense."

"So what now?" Stevie said.

"Go home and write," Kelleher said. "And then ask more questions tomorrow. I think it was Woodward who first said to me, 'Never think a story is over.' At some point every day you have to sit down and write, but you never stop trying to gather more information.

"So write what you know now. And then keep digging."

THE DEEP END

After a long talk with Stevie about his adventures at the Army-Navy lunch, Susan Carol decided she should start compiling her notes for the story they were supposed to write on the Secret Service's pregame security measures. The story had taken a turn for the weird, and she figured it'd help to have everything in order when they started to write.

But a quick check of her emails sent the thought of the security story right out of her head. The subject line was: *Letter to the Editor—Any comments?*

When she opened up the email, she found a note from the woman in charge of the letters page at the *Post*: *Thought you should see the attached. The plan is to run it on Thursday. If you have any comments, please let me know by early Wednesday.*

Susan Carol opened the attachment and let out a little gasp as she began to read:

I'm writing in regard to the story that appeared in Sunday morning's *Post* under the byline of Susan Carol Anderson. The story is misleading, it is false, and, in my opinion and those of our lawyers at the conference office, it is libelous. Ms. Anderson calls the officials who worked the Navy–Notre Dame game incompetents at best, cheaters at worst. She questions the honesty of referee Mike Daniels because he chose not to speak to a reporter. For the record, officials are *never* required to speak to the media, and only do so if there is a rule that needs interpreting. Mr. Daniels was simply following the policies he has been asked to follow. I'm extremely disappointed that the *Post* would publish a baseless and inflammatory story like this one. My understanding is that Ms. Anderson is fourteen years old and a high school freshman. Perhaps it is not surprising that when you substitute children for seasoned reporters, you end up with ill-informed, immature, and emotional stories rather than those grounded in fact. In printing it, you do a disservice both to my professionals and to your readers.

Yours truly,
Harold Neve, supervisor,
ACC football officials

Susan Carol reread the letter three times, getting a little angrier each time. And just a little bit scared.

She forwarded the email to Stevie and called him immediately.

"Miss me already?" he said, answering the phone.

"Go read your email," she said.

"What's up?"

"Just go read! I'll wait while you do."

"Okay, okay." She could hear clicking and then Stevie saying, "Whoa . . . whoa . . . WHOA!

"Gee, Susan Carol," he said, finally done reading. "Usually I'm the one to shoot off my mouth and get in trouble."

"I know, that's why I called—I figured you'd know what to do."

"Honestly? I usually do nothing and it blows over."

"But how can I say nothing? Did you see what he said? He called me a liar and said I'd committed libel and threatened to sue and—".

"Hang on, hang on," Stevie said. "The guy is clearly an idiot. Anyone who saw the game or the replays knows the officials screwed Navy. He's just trying to cover that up by complaining about you."

"And I suppose you'd be this calm if it were you they were calling a liar?"

He thought about that one for a second. "No, probably not. I'd be furious, like you. But then I'd also have you to calm me down."

"I guess. But, Stevie, people are going to read this and believe him."

"Maybe a few. But not anyone who saw the game. And certainly not anyone who knows you."

Susan Carol had to admit to herself that she and Stevie were spoiled. They'd gotten used to having people tell them how talented they were. This was the first time someone had publicly called her out on a story.

"So, you don't think I should respond?"

"That I don't know. See what Bobby and Tamara think."

When she spoke to them the next morning, Tamara was philosophical.

"Oh, Susan Carol, I'm sorry. But letters written by angry people are a part of the job. Harold Neve is writing so he can show all his referees, not just Daniels, that he backs them up when they get criticized."

"Even when they're wrong?" Susan Carol said.

"*Especially* when they're wrong," Tamara said. "Listen, you're going to get *hundreds* of these in your career. People are going to call you names, they're going to call you a liar, and sometimes they're going to say things about you that are completely untrue.

"I once wrote a story about a basketball coach who showed me a letter in which the president of his school promised to raise money to renovate and modernize their gym. When the story came out, the president told the coach if he didn't sign a letter to the editor saying no such letter had ever existed, he'd be fired."

"So what'd he do?"

"He signed the letter, then sent a copy of the president's original letter to my boss so he'd know I had it right, which was incredibly decent of him. But still, everyone who read the letter to the editor thought I'd somehow made the whole thing up."

"Wow," Susan Carol said. "I'd have wanted to kill that president."

"I did want to," Tamara said. "But you have to understand that when you tell the truth, there will be people who don't want to hear it. This is one of those times."

Kelleher took the phone then and said, "Really, Susan Carol. Don't sweat it. Harold Neve wrote almost the exact same letter about me eleven years ago. I wrote about that line judge who robbed Navy of certain victory by incorrectly moving the ball up a yard and giving Notre Dame a first down in the last minute. Neve wrote a letter questioning my integrity, my manhood, my breeding—everything. He never addressed the fact that his guy screwed up. This is the same thing. Notice he says nothing about the two calls, just that you're a bad guy for pointing them out."

Talking to them all made Susan Carol feel a little better. But only a little.

It seemed to Susan Carol that Thanksgiving Day would never end.

The only good news was that she and her mother would be leaving after dinner to drive across the state to Charlotte. One of the most important age-group swim meets of the early season was being held there on Friday morning, and Susan Carol would swim her two butterfly events—the 100 and the 200.

But she spent a lot of the day ducking her two obnoxious cousins and a busybody aunt.

She tried to hide out in the family room with her father, watching the Lions take their annual Thanksgiving mauling—this time from the Bears.

Her dad truly loved football. He had worked for a while as the team chaplain for the Carolina Panthers, and he ran clinics and support groups for people with all kinds of sports addictions. Susan Carol thought he was good at it because he understood—at least a little—how they felt.

But she couldn't even watch football—bad football at that—without flinching every time a ref's whistle blew.

"Suzy Q, you need to stop brooding about that letter," her father finally said.

She sighed—he could always read her.

"Do you believe what you wrote is true?" he asked.

"That's the thing. I keep second-guessing myself. They were terrible calls. There's no doubt about that. And I believe they should admit they got it wrong and not just dodge the blame by attacking me." She paused. "But I didn't really mean to accuse them of cheating, not literally. I was so mad when I wrote it, and I kind of thought the editor at the *Post* would cut out the harshest bits. . . ."

"But he didn't?"

"No, Matt Rennie said I'd really nailed them and that they deserved it."

"Hmm. I don't know what to tell you, then, sweetie. Next time, try not to write in anger. Words are powerful things. And they can be used to hurt as well as help."

"Kinda like penalty flags . . ."

"Huh," he snorted. "Yes, with great power comes great responsibility. . . ."

"Now you're making me Spider-Man!"

"You could do worse than to be a protector of the innocent."

They both laughed, and Susan Carol did feel better.

"Dad," she said a while later. "Say a ref really was cheating—how would he do it?"

"Susan.Carol. Don't decide they're guilty just because *you* feel guilty for accusing them. . . ."

"No, really, just hypothetically. I know you know about this stuff from your clinics."

"Well, hypothetically, I guess a ref could cheat by trying to affect the score of the game. There are lots of different ways to bet on football. The most obvious is to just pick the winner—but usually that involves odds. For example, if you wanted to bet the Bears to win straight up today, you'd probably have to give about five-to-one odds. That means if you win a dollar, the person you're betting with wins five if the Lions win."

"What else?" Susan Carol asked.

"Most people bet with the points because there are no odds involved," he said. "In this game, the Bears are favored, I think, by six and a half points. That means if you bet on the Lions and they lose the game by six points or less—or win, obviously—you win the bet. If the Bears win by seven points or more, the people betting on the Bears win. Sometimes a few points either way could make a big difference."

She nodded. "Okay. I know about that. I hear people say they're 'taking the points' all the time. But I also hear people say they bet the 'under.' What's the 'under'?"

He smiled. "You need to know everything, don't you? An 'over-under' bet is based on the total number of points scored in the game. The bookie—the person you place the bet with—sets the lines, the point spreads, all that. If he sets the 'over-under' number at, say, fifty points, then you have a choice: you can bet the 'under,' and if the two teams combined score fewer than fifty points, you win. If you bet the 'over,' and they score more than fifty points, you win."

"What if they score exactly fifty points?"

"It's a push—a tie," her father said. "No one wins, but the bookie collects the fee you pay to make the bet—usually ten percent."

"So the bookie is fine with a tie, then, right?"

"Absolutely. The bookie always finds a way to win. Which is why it's better not to bet. Along with it being illegal in most places."

Aunt Catherine poked her head in the door. "Football time is over," she said. "Time for dinner."

Dinner seemed to take forever, especially after Aunt Catherine decided she didn't think her brother's blessing was "adequate."

"I think we should be more thankful than that, don't you?" she said.

"I thought he was plenty thankful," her mom said.

"And I'm plenty hungry," her dad said.

Susan Carol was in the car with her mom, getting nervous about her swims the next morning, when she got a text from Stevie: *When u r done w/dinner call me.*

She called right away.

"Bobby just called," he said.

"On Thanksgiving?"

"Big sports day. Plus, he always works, you know that. Anyway, he said one of his political buddies has a source inside the White House who says there's talk about canceling the president's appearance at the game."

"Really?" she said.

"Yeah, and guess who Bobby wants to try to find out what's going on from the Secret Service?"

"Why us?" she said, not even bothering to answer the rhetorical question. "He's the one who's friends with those guys."

"He thinks we're less threatening."

"I guess we are," Susan Carol said.

"Well, I am, anyway. I know some officials who feel pretty darn threatened by you."

"Not funny!" Susan Carol said—though it kind of was.

"How are you doing, now that the letter is in print?" Stevie asked.

"Okay, I guess. I didn't mean to say they'd blown the game on purpose, really. But man, those were bad calls! I don't know how they got it so wrong."

"Well, shake it off; you've got a big meet tomorrow."

"Yeah, I know."

"Good luck. I hope that piano doesn't land on your back."

"Thanks for bringing it up." She snapped the phone shut.

Susan Carol had smiled when Stevie mentioned the piano, because she knew he was showing off his newfound knowledge of swimming. He had actually tried to learn more about her sport and had mostly patiently listened to what he not-so-patiently called her "geek talk" about it.

The scariest event going for any swimmer was the 200 butterfly. The 400 individual medley was exhausting, and you could really, really hurt swimming the 200 in any stroke because it wasn't a pure distance event or a pure sprint event. But there was nothing quite like the 200 'fly.

Butterfly was the only stroke in which it was possible for an in-shape, seasoned swimmer to not finish. You had to get both arms out of the water at the same time *and* get your body up out of the water far enough to complete each stroke. If you ran out of gas, it was entirely possible that you would not be able to get your arms out of the water at the finish. It was not an uncommon sight to see a butterflyer—even a good one—almost come to a stop five yards from the wall.

Every butterflyer who ever lived had a story about it. The lingo was, "Ten yards out, the piano landed on my back."

Stepping onto the blocks the next morning for the 200 'fly, Susan Carol wasn't thinking about the piano. She was thinking about keeping her stroke as smooth as possible, making sure not to over-kick the first 150 yards. She'd broken a minute in her 100 'fly, which was a good sign this early in the year, and now she wanted to make sure her 200 'fly was just as solid. She wasn't looking for spectacular—not in November anyway.

Susan Carol looked to her right, saw Becky Asmus, and reminded herself to ignore her once they were in the water. Susan Carol was tall and lean. Becky Asmus was built like a linebacker and so strong that no one in their age group could come close to her. An ideal time for Susan Carol in this race would be about 2:10, maybe 2:12. Asmus would be closer to 2:00. Susan Carol wanted nothing to do with her.

For one hundred yards, Susan Carol swam perfectly. Her stroke was smooth, and she was about a body length behind Asmus. She was a little surprised during the third fifty when Asmus appeared to be coming back to her. And even more when they were just about even at the 150-yard turn.

Either Asmus was swimming the slowest 200 'fly of her life, or Susan Carol had picked up her pace a little too much during the third fifty. Sure enough, she began to feel her arms tightening as she hit the wall at the 175. Asmus, predictably, was pulling away. That didn't bother her. The way her arms felt as she came up out of the last turn did.

KICK, she screamed to herself, knowing that was the only chance she had to keep from going vertical. She could see the flags ahead of her. If she could just get there, she could put her head down the last five yards and dive into the wall. But her arms were gone. The piano had landed.

STAY LEGAL was her new mantra the last ten yards. She did—her arms barely getting above the water. By her unofficial count she needed nine strokes for the last ten yards. Normally she needed nine strokes for an entire length of the pool.

She finally hit the wall and pulled her goggles up to look at the time. Her heart sank: 2:16.79. She had still finished second in the 13–14 age group, but the time made her want to punch something. Which she did, pounding the wall with her hand.

Coach Brennan put an arm around her when she got out of the pool. "The third fifty . . ."

"I know," she said.

"Okay," he said. "We won't talk about it now. Just make sure you get in the water and work hard on your own the next few days while you're away."

She nodded. She went into the showers and burst into tears. No one, except another butterflyer, could know how much that piano hurt.

SOURCES AND RESOURCES

By Saturday, Susan Carol had mostly shaken off her bad swim and the letter to the editor. Or at least put them in the back of her mind. She was too busy to brood. Stevie was running down the schedule for their afternoon at West Point.

"The team practices at three o'clock. We're seeing Coach Ellerson in his office at one thirty, and Tamara's talking to the superintendent at two. We've got to write some kind of story, maybe two, for the Sunday papers after practice. They'll really start gearing up the coverage in the Sunday papers."

Susan Carol nodded. "And what about the security story?"

"Bobby wanted us to talk to either Dowling or Campbell—if they're here—and see if we can confirm his source's tip that the president might not come. Oh, and find out why not, of course."

"Sure, no problem."

When they arrived at Ellerson's office, the receptionist said, "You guys are right on time. The only problem is, Coach isn't. He's in a meeting right now, but I'm sure he'll be with you just as soon as possible."

So they waited. Twenty minutes later, they saw two men walking down the hallway in their direction. One was Rich Ellerson. The other was Pete Dowling.

"Hey, Steve, you got out of the dining room at the Linc," Dowling said, smiling as everyone shook hands.

Stevie introduced Susan Carol to Ellerson and Dowling.

"So am I guessing that you being here means the president is still coming to the game?" Susan Carol said, flashing The Smile to try to make the question sound like "What time is sunset?" rather than something more serious.

If the question bothered Dowling, he didn't show it. "Don't believe everything Bobby Kelleher tells you," he said. "I saw that story in the *Herald* this morning. His guy got a bad tip. The president's coming. I think everyone's jumping at shadows a little bit because of what happened Tuesday."

"Fraternity prank," Stevie said.

"Odd but true," Dowling said. "And now everyone's putting two and two together and getting five."

"So you aren't worried about anything?" Susan Carol asked.

Dowling laughed. "I worry about everything," he said. "That's my job."

"Will you be around today?" Susan Carol asked.

"All day," Dowling said. "Maybe I'll see you at practice."

They shook hands and Ellerson waved them into his office, which had a great view overlooking the stadium, the field, the reservoir, and the wooded hills beyond.

"We may not be able to recruit too many NFL prospects here," Ellerson said as they sat down. "But I wouldn't trade my office with any coach in the country."

Stevie could see why. It was spacious, and the view was spectacular.

"Does all this Secret Service stuff bother you?" Susan Carol asked once they were seated. "I mean, is it a distraction?"

"For the players, I'd say no. The older guys on the team have been through this before. For me, it's a first, so it adds some time and detail I could probably live without. But it's part of the deal here at Army. And it's an honor to have the president attend. I'm just disappointed the vice president isn't coming. I'm told he's a big Army fan. The president will be more neutral."

Stevie looked at Susan Carol. They had been told from the start that Vice President Biden was going to attend with President Obama. This was the first they'd heard about the VP not coming.

"So Biden's not coming?" Susan Carol said to confirm.

"Apparently not," Ellerson said. He paused. "Oh, I probably shouldn't have told you that. Do me a favor and don't use that unless you hear it from Agent Dowling. He was pretty firm that I wasn't supposed to say anything about our meeting, and I didn't realize word wasn't out about Biden."

"It might be," Stevie said. "It's probably common knowledge and we just hadn't heard it yet."

Ellerson nodded. "Yeah, probably. I guess they're always a little hesitant about the two of them being in the same place. . . ."

"And after Tuesday . . . ," Susan Carol said.

Ellerson held up a hand. "Let's talk football, okay? This isn't my area of expertise."

The next forty minutes were entertaining. Ellerson knew a lot of Army-Navy lore, especially since his father and uncle were both graduates. His uncle had been captain of the 1962 team, and Ellerson clearly had a long-standing love of the place.

"You know, Jim Platt, one of our assistant basket-ball coaches, may have described it best," he told them. "He said, 'Coaching the kids who come here is never easy, but it sure is fun to try.' Most aren't naturally gifted, but to say they'd run through a wall for you isn't hyper-bole."

He filled them in on some of the team's most story-worthy players: three players had brothers deployed in either Iraq or Afghanistan. One had a cousin who had been killed in Iraq. Many came from military families and considered the five years in the military after graduation a calling more than an obligation.

Stevie was truly sorry when it was time to go. "Anything comes up, call me," Ellerson said, giving them both his cell number. "Only thing I ask in return is you protect me on the Biden thing."

Stevie and Susan Carol walked around the post a bit before practice started, but it was cold and gray, and a light mist was falling, so it wasn't the scenic stroll Stevie had been imagining. And standing on the sidelines wasn't much nicer.

"Why can't they practice inside?" Susan Carol said. "It's like thirty-five degrees out here—maybe."

"Last I knew, the game's being played outdoors," Stevie said.

But he felt bad when he saw Susan Carol shivering.

He found Bob Beretta, the Army sports information director, and asked if he could go inside and ask Dick Hall for a hat for Susan Carol.

Beretta smiled. "Of course. Dicky will give you all the warm clothing that you want. If someone else stops you, just tell them I sent you to Dicky."

Hall was working on a player's helmet when Stevie walked in.

"See if that feels better, Ronnie," he said.

The player moved his head from side to side. "Much better," he said. "Thanks, Mr. Hall."

Hall gave him a pat on the shoulder as he headed for the field. Seeing Stevie, Hall broke into a wide grin. "Well, if it isn't our own Bob Woodward," he said.

Stevie laughed. "Yes—and Bernstein's outside, and she's freezing. I was hoping you could spare a couple of those warm stocking caps."

"Follow me," Hall said.

He veered into his office for a moment and began tossing candy packages at Stevie from a large bowl. Once Stevie's hands were full, he led him into a room off the locker room that was filled with every imaginable piece of football equipment—helmets, shoulder pads, jerseys, pants, sweats, and caps. He stopped in front of a shelf near the back and pulled a box down.

He picked two black and gold ski caps that said ARMY out of the box and tossed them to Stevie. "Two enough?" he said. "Need anything else?"

Stevie wouldn't have minded grabbing one of everything—except maybe the shoulder pads and helmets—but he shook his head. "No thanks," he said. Then thought again. "Well, maybe some information? I think the Secret Service is nervous about next Saturday. And I have a feeling you may know for sure."

Hall's smile faded. "Why would I know?" he asked.

"Because you're the guy around here who knows everything," Stevie said. "Am I right?"

"You're half right," Hall said. "Come with me."

He led him through the locker room and into the

training room and knocked on the door to an office in the back.

Hall pushed the door open and Stevie saw Tim Kelly at his desk doing some paperwork. He smiled when he looked up and saw Stevie.

"Couldn't stay away, could you?" he said.

"Our friend is looking for some help," Hall said.

"You hurt?" Kelly asked. "Everything okay? Should I get one of our docs?"

"No, no, I'm fine, thanks," Stevie said. "But I was asking Mr. Hall what was going on with the Secret Service and he brought me to you. I figure you're the people who know what's really going on around here."

"You're right," said Kelly. "That's what the Secret Service thought too."

DIDN'T SEE *THAT* COMING

Tim Kelly explained why the Secret Service had sought him and Dick Hall out. "On any football team, the people who know the players the best are the trainer and the equipment manager."

"Not their position coach?" Stevie asked.

Hall jumped in. "There are things kids keep from their coaches because they're afraid it might affect their playing time: a fight with their girlfriend, a minor injury, feeling sick a couple days before a game, something going on with their parents at home. There's lots of stuff."

"To be honest, it's especially true here because Dicky and I have been around a long time," Kelly said. "When Bob Sutton was the coach here, he would say that visiting grads *sometimes* went to the football office to say hello, but they *always* went to the equipment room or the training room."

"They like my candy," Hall joked.

"So the Secret Service came to you guys wanting to know what? If there was anyone on the team who might want to hurt the president?" Stevie said.

"No, no. But they were interested in anyone who might be connected with a hate group, or a white supremacy group, or know someone who was."

"Whoa. Do you know if they had some specific reason for asking?"

"No, no idea. They made it seem routine. . . ."

"And—is that something a player would actually tell you?"

"Possibly," Kelly said. "We *have* had white players in the past who weren't that comfortable playing with blacks. Some came from all-white teams in high school. They got over it pretty fast. To be honest, if there's a bias issue in this locker room—or in almost any football locker room—it's against gays."

"Huh. Do you have gay players?" Stevie asked, even though he was going off topic.

Kelly shrugged. "I'm sure we have. Statistics say we have. But if you think the military is 'don't ask, don't tell,' try a football locker room."

Stevie thought that was interesting but tried to steer the conversation back to the topic at hand. "So the Secret Service came to you and . . . ?"

"They had pulled *everyone's* file before they came to see us," Kelly said. "Mostly they asked routine stuff to confirm what was there or amplify on it a little. The guys they asked the most about seemed to be from the South, and some did come from all-white programs. That's who they were interested in."

"And is there anyone you were worried about?" Stevie asked.

"Absolutely not," Kelly said. "There's nothing that we know of to be concerned about. And we probably *would* know."

"I guess they're doing the same thing at Navy," Stevie said.

"I imagine they're doing the same thing with anyone and everyone who might come in contact with the president," Hall said. He sighed. "Look, nothing's wrong here, really. It just makes me uncomfortable to be thinking about people in this way—to look at everyone like a potential suspect. Especially these kids. Asking about the Southerners is a form of profiling, as far as I'm concerned."

Stevie nodded. "I know what you mean. Thanks for helping me out."

"One more thing," Kelly said.

"What's that?" Stevie asked.

"Do us a favor and forget you ever talked to us."

Susan Carol was standing with Bob Beretta on the 40-yard line when Stevie came trotting out of the locker room.

"What'd you do, take a hot shower while you were in there?" Susan Carol asked.

"Almost," Stevie said, handing her the ski cap, which she gratefully pulled over her head. "Mr. Hall is a great storyteller."

Beretta laughed. "You've certainly got that right. If there's anything you want to know about any Army football player of the last forty years, Dicky is definitely the man to see."

Susan Carol was giving him a look that said, "Something's up and you aren't telling me." He gave her a look back that he hoped conveyed, "You're right, I'll tell you later."

Beretta was pointing out players he thought they might want to talk to when practice was over: Trent Steelman, the sophomore quarterback who had taken over the job from day one as a freshman; Jared Hassin, the bruising fullback who had transferred from the Air Force Academy—a rarity—and Michael Arnott, whose older brother played at Navy.

"There really are so many good stories here, it's hard to choose just one or two," Susan Carol said.

Tim Kelly came out and joined them as the practice wore on. Kathy Orton from the *Post*, who had come up to spend a couple of days with Army in search of some offbeat stories, was also there. Tamara must have still been with the superintendent.

"The only real question when you're writing about these two teams is who *not* to write about," Orton said, shivering. "Every one of these kids has a story to tell."

"How tall are you?" Susan Carol said, a complete non sequitur except for the fact that Orton was just about as tall as Susan Carol.

"I'm five eleven," Orton said. "You?"

"Same," Susan Carol said, though when Stevie stepped back to look, he thought Susan Carol seemed taller. "Does it help to be tall when you're a female sportswriter?" Susan Carol asked.

"Actually, I think it does," Orton said. "I think it makes it less intimidating talking to athletes. Only a few are a *lot* taller than I am, and that's mostly in basketball."

"I guess it's not as bad when you're an adult," Susan Carol said.

Orton laughed. "I feel your pain," she said. "I've been this height since I was your age."

Susan Carol smiled. "Well, maybe if I'm lucky, I won't grow any more."

"Maybe if *I'm* lucky, you won't grow any more," Steve said, jumping in.

"Come on, Stevie, I like you just the way you are," Susan Carol said. "Hey, watch out!"

While they had been gabbing on about everyone's height, the Army offense had snapped the ball from a few yards away and had run a pitch play in their direction. Stevie looked up and saw one of the running backs bearing down on him with two defenders trying to push their teammate out of bounds. He jumped back, but it was too late. The running back crashed into him and the two of them fell—with the running back landing directly on top of Stevie.

"You okay?" he heard the runner say.

"Yeah, think so," Stevie said, although he was feeling a bit woozy and his head hurt from hitting it on the ground.

"Let me get a look at him, Jared. Steve, don't try to get up. Just lie still."

Stevie saw Tim Kelly swim into view as he knelt down beside him and heard Jared's voice behind him, asking, "Is he okay, Mr. Kelly? I couldn't stop. I didn't mean to . . ."

"I think so," Kelly said. "Get on back to the huddle. I'll take care of him."

Jared leaned down and patted Stevie on the shoulder. "Really sorry, man," he said.

"I should have seen you," Stevie said, just as a jolt of pain went through his arm.

Kelly saw him wince. "Where's it hurt?" he asked.

"My arm."

"How's your head?" he asked. "Can you tell me what day it is, where we are?"

Stevie almost laughed. "It's Saturday afternoon, we're at West Point, it's freezing, and Susan Carol and Kathy are both three inches taller than I am. Susan Carol, maybe four."

Kelly smiled. "Okay, good. Let's get you up and take a look at that arm."

He helped Stevie to his feet. As he did, pain shot through Stevie's left arm and he almost doubled over.

Susan Carol, Orton, and Beretta were all gathered around. And Coach Ellerson had come over to check on him too.

"Everything okay, Tim?" Ellerson asked.

"Well, he never lost consciousness, and he's not groggy at all," Kelly said. "But he seems to have hurt his arm. I'm going to take him inside and have a look."

Ellerson nodded. "Okay, let me know how it goes. Really sorry, Steve."

Stevie tried to force a smile. "Should have been paying better attention," he said.

He and Kelly turned to head to the locker room. Susan Carol asked Kelly if she could go with them.

"Sure," Kelly said.

They walked slowly inside, Kelly supporting Stevie's throbbing arm.

"Did I break it?" he asked.

"I need to get a look," Kelly said. "We may have to do an X-ray to be sure. Let's not panic just yet."

Stevie was panicking. The last thing he needed right now was a broken arm.

"Assuming you're right-handed, you might have gotten a little bit lucky," Kelly said.

Before Stevie could answer, Susan Carol jumped in. "He's a lefty."

"So maybe you weren't so lucky," Kelly said.

They made it inside the training room, and Kelly helped Stevie up onto a table after carefully taking his jacket off. He unbuttoned Stevie's shirt for him and helped him get it off too.

"Okay, I'm going to feel around a little bit and move your arm around a little bit," Kelly said. "You just let me know when it hurts."

Just about any movement hurt, as it turned out. Kelly kept apologizing but kept moving the arm up, then down, then out, then in toward his chest—which *really* hurt.

"Broken?" Susan Carol asked.

"Don't think so," Kelly said. "I'd like to try something, Steve, but I'll warn you in advance, it's gonna hurt."

"What's that?" Stevie asked.

"Just trust me for a minute and then I'll explain," Kelly said. "Susan Carol, do me a favor and stand on Steve's right and talk to him about something he likes. Steve, look at Susan Carol and focus on what she's talking about. I'm going to feel around here for another few seconds while you talk."

Stevie was baffled but did as he was told.

He felt Kelly taking ahold of his arm—which hurt— while Susan Carol began talking. "Mr. Beretta told me there's a great place nearby called Loughran's where they have a terrific prime rib," she said, picking Stevie's favorite topic—food.

"OH MY GOD!" Stevie screamed in pain. Kelly had just yanked on his arm so hard Stevie was convinced the trainer had pulled his arm out of its socket.

"What in the world did you do?" Susan Carol asked, her southern accent in full voice as it usually was when she was upset.

Kelly held up a hand. "I'm sorry that hurt so much. But

do me a favor, Steve: bend your arm, see how close to your face you can get your hand."

Stevie gave him a look, wondering what in the world made him think he could bend his arm. But he tried it anyway. He brought his hand up to his face and felt absolutely no pain. He did it a few times to be sure. He shook his arm to see if that hurt. There was still a little pain from where Kelly had yanked, but nothing like he felt before.

"Any pain?" Kelly asked.

"No, not really," Stevie said.

Kelly smiled. "My guess was right. You dislocated the elbow when you fell; that's why your arm was crooked the way it was. It looks like I was able to pop it back into place."

"Mr. Kelly, you are a genius!" Susan Carol said, The Smile lighting up her face, the southern accent there now because she was so pleased.

"I'm just a trainer," Kelly said. "I'm glad that's all it was. Now, Steve, if you feel any pain at all the next few days, you go see a doctor," Kelly continued. "I don't think you will, but—"

He stopped as the phone on the wall next to the table Stevie was sitting on rang. He looked at the caller ID screen and said, "Wonder what this could be?" He picked up the phone and said, "Jeff, what's up?"

For the next few moments, he listened, his face showing increasing concern. Finally, he said, "Really? A positive connection? With the who?" He nodded. "Okay, thanks for the heads-up. I imagine that's what they'll do here. Let's stay in touch."

He hung up and looked at Stevie and Susan Carol. "That was Jeff Fair, who is my counterpart at Navy," he said.

"I met him at Notre Dame," Susan Carol said.

Kelly nodded. "Yeah. Good guy . . ." He trailed off.

• "That sounded . . . important," Stevie offered.

"I don't know, I'm just shocked. Apparently the Secret Service has found a connection between a player's family and a hate group."

"Really? Did he say who?" asked Susan Carol.

Kelly blinked a couple times and shook his head. "I'm sorry. I shouldn't have said anything. This is . . . Steve, if you're feeling better, let's get back out to the field, okay?"

SURPRISING INTERVIEWS

"I heard you took quite a hit," Dowling said as Stevie, Susan Carol, and Kelly walked up.

"He dislocated his elbow," Kelly said. "I was able to pop it back in."

"Stevie was very brave," Susan Carol put in.

Tamara had returned from her interview with the supe. "Stevie! I leave you two alone for two hours . . . ," she teased, clearly relieved that he seemed okay.

More media members had also shown up. There were a couple of TV crews, but they weren't filming anything, apparently at Ellerson's request. Beretta introduced Stevie and Susan Carol to two columnists who had joined the group shivering in the rain: Mike Vaccaro from the *New York Post* and Kevin Gleason from the *Times Herald-Record,* the local paper that, Stevie knew from reading clips, covered Army more thoroughly than anyone.

"It is such a pleasure to meet you both," Susan Carol said. "Mr. Vaccaro, I just *loved* your book on the World Series."

Dowling turned to Beretta and said, "Bob, did you explain to these guys that I'm going to need a couple of your kids as soon as practice is over?"

"Didn't get the chance yet," Beretta said. "I'm sure they understand."

"It's just some background stuff we're finishing up," Dowling said. "Pretty routine. Won't take long."

"I think the media request who is on your list, Pete, is Mike Arnott," Beretta said. "The rest of the guys the media needs you've already talked to. Kathy and Susan Carol wanted to talk to Mike. I'll get you two in with Derek Klein while you're waiting."

Stevie noticed that Ellerson had blown his whistle and all the players were making their way toward the middle of the field.

"Is it okay if I go listen?" Stevie asked.

"Sure," Beretta said. "I doubt if he's going to keep them long in this weather."

Stevie trotted onto the field, followed by Gleason.

"I'll represent the old guys," Gleason said.

The players had gathered around Ellerson. Most took a knee, Stevie noticing that the artificial turf field—which looked at first glance like real grass—hadn't gotten too wet.

"Fellas, if the weather is like this tomorrow, we'll go inside," Ellerson said. "We want to know what bad weather feels like, but we also don't want anyone getting sick. That was a good workout today." He glanced in Stevie's direction and said, "Mr. Thomas, I'm glad to see you look to be okay. Jared, that's one less member of the media who will write anything bad about you."

Everyone laughed.

Ellerson went on. "There are seven of you who Mr. Dowling from the Secret Service needs to see today just to go over some paperwork issues. I know it's a pain, but these guys are just doing a job—a tough one at that. So, once you've showered, I need Conroy, Calame, Parker, Klein, Thompson, Arnott, and Davis to report to Mr. Hall's office. Mr. Dowling will talk to each of you there. He won't need more than a few minutes.

"Same time tomorrow. And, fellas: I know it's Saturday, I know you can sleep in tomorrow, but let's not get carried away tonight. One week from today we'll be playing Navy. Remember that."

They huddled up, hands in, and on the count of three said, "Beat Navy!"

Then they all began sprinting for the locker room, wanting to get inside as fast as possible.

Stevie and Gleason returned to the others on the sideline.

"Anything gripping?" Vaccaro asked.

"Yeah," Gleason said. "I've learned exclusively that they want to beat Navy."

But Stevie did have something. He had a list of seven

names the Secret Service was interested in—perhaps in more than a routine way.

As everyone headed to the locker room, Stevie felt an arm on his shoulders.

"Hey, I just wanted to be sure you're okay."

Stevie looked up and saw Jared Hassin, the running back who had barreled into him.

"I'm fine," he said. "I guess my elbow got dislocated when I hit the ground. Mr. Kelly popped it back in."

"Glad to hear it," Hassin said. "I'm really sorry, man. I saw you, I just couldn't stop."

"No, no, it was my fault," Stevie said. "I wasn't paying enough attention."

They shook hands and Hassin trotted off. It was really tough not to like *all* these guys.

He followed the media group inside. Coach Ellerson was going to be in an interview room right away, and the players who had been requested by media would be available after they showered and changed.

"Trent said he needs about fifteen minutes," Bob Baretta said, seeing Stevie as he walked in. "It will be you and Mike Vaccaro."

Stevie had asked to interview quarterback Trent Steelman—but he was happy for a few minutes to think first. His head was swimming with half-formed theories and questions.

He decided to use the time to call Kelleher. Telling Bobby helped him order his thoughts on it all.

"So what did Kelly say on the phone? 'A positive connection'?"

"Right. But . . . just because someone belongs to a hate group—or knows someone who does—it doesn't mean they have plans to *do* anything. . . ."

"True, you're right. But clearly the Secret Service is taking it seriously."

"This security story is starting to feel a little too real," Stevie said.

"I know," Kelleher said. "But the Secret Service and the FBI know what they're doing, especially when it comes to protecting the president. They don't mess around."

"So what do we do now?" Stevie asked.

"Get your interviews done and write today's stories," Kelleher said. "Write what you know now—"

"I know," finished Stevie, "and keep digging."

Not surprisingly, Trent Steelman was bright, engaging, and funny. He got Stevie's attention right away when he mentioned that he had been eleven years old the last time Army had beaten Navy. Stevie did a little math and realized that he had been *six* the last time Army had won the game.

He asked Steelman how he and his teammates felt about President Obama coming to the game. Steelman smiled.

"Well, on the one hand, it's a thrill," he said. "I think

we're all looking forward to meeting him, getting a chance to shake hands with him. He's the commander in chief. . . ."

He paused. Vaccaro jumped in. "But," he said.

Steelman shrugged. "To be honest, the whole security thing is wearing us out a little," he said. "We all understand it, but they told us that when we get to the stadium, we're all going to have to get off the bus, get wanded, have the bus checked, and only then will they let us drive into the tunnel. Like I said, I *get* it, but we're just trying to get ready to play a football game. One none of us have ever won."

Stevie understood. He liked Steelman's honesty.

"I know you guys get asked this all the time," he said. "But can you talk about what it's like to be a student and an athlete here?"

"You mean what's it like to try juggle steak knives with one hand while shooting a rifle with the other?" Steelman asked, smiling.

"It's hard," he continued. "It's hard every day. One of the sayings among the cadets is that this is a great place to be *from* but not a great place to be.

"But I actually like that it's hard. I think all of us—at least all of us who stay—feel that way. We get up early, we can't miss class, we can get into trouble for almost anything. The other day one of the guys got put on report because he got caught riding an elevator in the barracks between classes. He had knee surgery two months ago, so he sneaks onto the elevator every now and then.

"But we all chose this. And going through the same tough experience together really forms a bond. So being here? Playing with these guys and under these amazing coaches? This is the easiest part of my week. The best part of my week."

"Even on a cold wet practice like today?"

"Oh yeah, even today. No—maybe especially today. Because it's so close, this game we've been working toward. We're almost there. And we're ready."

At that moment, Susan Carol and Kathy Orton were being introduced to Michael Arnott. The first thing Susan Carol noticed was that they were both taller than he was. Linebackers at the military academies came in considerably different sizes, she thought, than they did at the big-time schools.

Arnott was wearing his gray winter uniform, had wavy blond hair, and was, Susan Carol thought, quite handsome. He had an easygoing manner and apologized for making the two reporters wait. "I had to talk to the Secret Service, really sorry."

"Not exactly your fault," Kathy said.

Arnott smiled. "True enough," he said as they all sat down.

Susan Carol noticed he had a southern accent. "Sounds like you're a southerner like me," she said.

"I'm from Sumter, South Carolina."

"Nice weather to practice in today, huh?"

Arnott laughed. "After four years at this place, you almost don't notice it anymore."

They talked for a while about the game, about how much Army wanted to break the losing streak against Navy, and how having a brother there—and a younger brother at that—made the rivalry all the more intense.

What Susan Carol really wanted to know was what the Secret Service had asked him, so she was pleased when Orton moved the discussion away from football. "This is the first time President Obama's been to the game," she said. "Are you guys looking forward to that?"

Susan Carol watched Arnott closely, checking his face and his body language.

"Anytime the president comes, it's a big deal," he said. "I know we're all hoping to shake his hand. I know for me, I'll always remember that the first time I pulled a lever in a presidential election, it was for President Obama. So it will be exciting to actually meet him. But I think my roommate, Adrian Calame, is even more excited. We've talked a lot about what it means to him and to other African Americans to have an African American in the White House. It's cool to feel part of a time when the country is changing—and to be a part of that change."

Orton asked, "Being here at the academy and in the north, have you found racial attitudes a little bit different than where you grew up?"

Arnott nodded. "To put it mildly," he said. "I grew up in an all-white neighborhood and got sent to an all-white private school when I was in the sixth grade. So I competed *against* black players in high school but never with one until I got here. My parents and a lot of their friends are from a generation that hasn't quite outgrown a lot of the traditions of the old South. I argue with them all the time about whether the Confederate flag should fly over the statehouse in South Carolina."

"So how did your parents feel when you told them you'd voted for President Obama?" Susan Carol asked.

Arnott smiled ruefully. "My dad told me I was an idiot. But that's part of what I mean about things changing. My dad said that it was one of the saddest days in American history. But I think it was one of our best."

When Stevie and Susan Carol compared notes after their interviews, things were as murky as before.

"Michael Arnott did say his dad was upset about the election, so I guess there could be something there. And since his brother is at Navy, what Kelly said about the Secret Service doing the same thing at both schools could mean they were talking to Alan Arnott too. . . ."

"We're guessing, though."

"Totally. Well," Susan Carol said, "we've got security questions, so I guess we should talk to our Secret Service contact."

"But how can we ask when we're not supposed to know any of this?"

"Carefully."

They found Dicky Hall outside his office.

"Is Mr. Dowling still in there?" Stevie asked.

Hall nodded. "He's with Joel Davis. Should be almost finished—he said I could have my office back about now."

Just then, the door to his office opened and Joel Davis walked out. Dowling was gathering up papers spread in front of him on Hall's desk.

"All done, Dick," he said. "Thanks for letting me use the office."

"No problem," Hall said.

"Could we talk for a minute, Mr. Dowling?" Susan Carol asked.

Dowling looked at his watch. "Sure, I've got a minute."

Hall stepped back to let Stevie and Susan Carol walk inside. And pulled the door shut behind them.

"What's up, guys?" Dowling asked.

"We're not sure—but it's starting to feel like *something*," Stevie began.

Dowling raised an eyebrow.

"Well, we know you guys were a little concerned about what happened in Philadelphia. . . ."

"Fraternity prank," Dowling said.

"As you keep saying. But then rumors started about the president not coming—"

"Rumors that are untrue," Dowling cut in.

"But now we hear Vice President Biden's not coming," said Susan Carol.

"Where did you hear *that*?"

"And now you've found some kind of connection

between a player and a hate group . . . ," Susan Carol continued.

"What?!" Dowling was clearly getting agitated.

"And today you had more follow-up questions for seven players—"

"Totally routine," Dowling interrupted.

"And one of those players was Michael Arnott, who I just interviewed with Kathy Orton. . . ."

Dowling was quiet now, so Susan Carol kept going. "And he happened to mention that his father was very upset about the election."

"How did he *happen* to mention that? I hope you haven't been sharing these . . . speculations of yours with—"

"No! Of course not," Susan Carol rushed to say. "Kathy was asking how he felt about meeting the president, same as we've been asking everyone."

"And we are working on a story about security at the game—you know that," Stevie added.

Dowling sighed. "Yes, but right now, I wish you weren't."

"Because we're right about this?" Susan Carol asked—a little surprised.

"No, because I'm afraid you're going to chase after these rumors and ideas you've got and make my job harder."

"Well," Stevie offered, "if you filled us in on what's going on, we'd be less likely to do that. . . ."

"No." Dowling was firm. "In my job, people tell *me* what *they* know, not the other way around.

"Now, I know that neither of your papers would print a story based on the kind of flimsy conjectures you've got going. And I will ask you both to please tread lightly on this and let the Secret Service do their job unimpeded.

"I'll be speaking to Bobby Kelleher about this—I suggest you do the same."

Susan Carol and Stevie exchanged a look as Dowling picked up his papers and briefcase and strode from the room.

One week before the Army-Navy game, and something was officially up.

GAME DAY: 38 MINUTES BEFORE KICKOFF

"**L**adies and gentlemen," the PA announcer said, "Mike Daniels and his team of officials for today's game will now present awards to the twelve winners of the second annual Outstanding Officials program. These twelve men were selected from around the country to be honored for their years of dedicated work as high school football referees."

As the PA guy droned on, introducing all twelve winners, Daniels presented each with a plaque as he congratulated them.

"Pretty ironic," Stevie said to Susan Carol.

She nodded but said, "It really is a hard job—"

"Stop feeling guilty!" Stevie said. "It's a hard job that four of those guys out there did really badly. And you said so. You told the truth."

Susan Carol nodded. "Let's hope they do better today."

"Everyone will be watching, that's for sure."

As the officials were all leaving the field, Stevie noticed Agent Dowling had his hand on his earpiece. "Copy that," he said into his wrist. Then he said to all of them, "Marine One has landed; the president is on his way to greet the teams in their locker rooms."

At last, Susan Carol thought. So much planning and preparing and strife, but it was really happening. The president was here.

She noticed that a group of midshipmen were now standing at attention at midfield facing a group of cadets.

"What's this?" she asked.

"Prisoner exchange," Kelleher said. "The mids have been exchange students at West Point this semester, and the cadets have been at Annapolis."

They all watched as the two groups saluted each other. Then the two lines stepped toward each other and for a moment blended into one. Then they kept going, the cadets heading toward the Army stands and the mids heading for Navy. Soon the lines grew wavy and then each group broke into a run—diving into the stands with their classmates.

"I guess they don't do anything like that at Michigan–Ohio State," Stevie said.

Kelleher laughed. "You've got that right," he said.

Next, the color guard marched into place at center field, and the PA announcer introduced the Reverend John Lotz to deliver the pregame prayer. Stevie wondered how it was possible to be both tense and bored at the same time. They were so close to things really starting, but this was taking forever!

Once the prayer was over, it was time for the national anthem. Stevie couldn't help but notice that almost everyone in the stadium was standing and singing. He remembered his dad once saying at an Eagles game that the reason almost no one sang the anthem was because most of the fans didn't know the words. So here was another way Army-Navy was special. Here, *everyone* knew the words and felt good about singing them loud and proud.

ON THE YARD

They were on the road to Annapolis by eleven o'clock. Saturday's rain had cleared, and it was a beautiful, breezy end-of-fall Sunday. They drove right through downtown, Kelleher giving them an informal tour that ended down by the docks, where boats were still tied up even with winter fast approaching. Soon Kelleher turned right into what was labeled GATE 1 at the Naval Academy.

Kelleher had some kind of special pass that allowed him to park on the academy grounds. "This place is a lot smaller than the Post is up at Army," he explained after they had been waved on through by the marine posted at the gate. "After 9/11, they banned all civilian traffic unless you had a special pass."

"How'd you get one?" Stevie asked.

"I know the guy who does their radio broadcasts."

Stevie wasn't surprised. When it came to parking, Kelleher always seemed to know *someone*.

They drove no more than a few hundred yards up the road until it curved left at the water's edge. Stevie could see downtown Annapolis directly across the water to the right. Kelleher swung the car into a small parking lot marked RICKETTS HALL and parked in a spot that said ATHLETIC DIRECTOR on it.

"Chet won't mind," Kelleher said, referring to Navy AD Chet Gladchuk. "He's got a Yard pass—he can park on the sidewalk if he wants. Come on, let's go find Scott Strasemeier and get the show on the road. We need to get a lot done today."

Almost on cue, the front door to Ricketts Hall opened and a man of about forty came walking out.

"Scott, we were just talking about you," Kelleher said as he walked up.

"At your service, as ever," the Navy sports information director replied.

They told him who everyone wanted to talk to and he nodded, taking it all in. Susan Carol interviewing Alan Arnott after practice would be no problem. "You know Kenny, he'll give you all the time you need," Strasemeier said to Kelleher. Getting Stevie time with Ricky Dobbs would be a little more complicated because all the TV people wanted to talk to him too, but he'd work him in.

"Meanwhile, we're flooded with Secret Service guys today," Strasemeier added. "They're all over on the practice field. Oh—Susan Carol, the Secret Service have a meeting with Alan Arnott after practice, so we'll get you to him right after."

While they talked, a number of players walked past them in their practice gear en route to the field. And to Stevie, it seemed that every last one of them stopped to say hello to Susan Carol.

"Thawed out yet?" said one who Stevie recognized as quarterback Ricky Dobbs.

"Just barely," Susan Carol answered, giving him The Smile.

"Did you get to know the *whole* team out at Notre Dame?" Stevie asked.

"Only about half of them," Tamara answered before Susan Carol could say anything.

They followed Strasemeier toward the practice field. A large gaggle of media were already out there, about twice the contingent that had been at Army the day before. Stevie was a little surprised to see that many people on a Sunday when the Redskins were playing.

"The Redskins are in Detroit," Kelleher said, doing his mind-reading thing. "They're also lousy. So not as many people made the trip out there. If the Redskins were any good, half these guys wouldn't be here."

One of the TV guys was approaching them. Stevie knew he was a TV guy because he was wearing a suit, and a print or radio guy wouldn't be caught dead in a suit at noon on a Sunday.

"Hello, everyone, nice to see you," the TV guy said. He turned to Stevie and Susan Carol. "Bret Haber from

Channel Nine in Washington," he said. "We met at the World Series."

That's where he'd seen him, Stevie remembered.

"So, Bobby, you're the smart one; what's with all the Secret Service up here for practice?" Haber said, nodding across the field, where Stevie could see Pete Dowling and several other guys in suits all wearing sunglasses with their arms folded.

"Good question," Kelleher said. "It might be one of those weird situations where the best way to find out is to ask."

Haber grunted. "I know I'm just a TV guy, so you may not believe this, but I already thought of that. I *did* ask."

"And . . ."

"And I was told to call the public information office if I wanted any comment."

"Maybe they've seen your work."

"Funny," Haber said. "I suppose you'll have better luck with them."

"Doubt it," Kelleher said. "They've probably seen my work too."

It was apparent to Stevie that, even though Kelleher and Haber were friends, Kelleher wasn't going to fill him in, even a little bit.

Haber laughed, waved a hand, and headed back to his camera crew.

"So, do we think it's significant that Agent Dowling is here to speak to Alan Arnott?" Susan Carol asked as they watched him pull out his phone.

Just then, Bobby's phone started to ring in his pocket. He looked at it and raised his eyebrows. "It would seem so," he said as he answered. He listened for a minute, then said, "Fine. Ten minutes."

He snapped the phone shut. "He'd like to meet us outside, by the water, in ten minutes."

Tamara suggested, rather loudly, that she and Bobby should give Stevie and Susan Carol a tour of the Yard since they'd never been there, and they all headed away from the field toward the water.

Susan Carol was so preoccupied that she barely noticed how pretty it all was. There were boats chugging in and out of the harbor. She could see the Chesapeake Bay Bridge, which stretched across the bay, connecting Annapolis and the rest of Maryland to the state's eastern shore.

But she couldn't focus on the sights at all. Playing cat and mouse with the Secret Service wasn't the reason she had gotten involved in sportswriting.

She loved to write. She loved sports. She love watching the practices up close and the games from the sidelines. She loved the camaraderie of the other writers.

And she really loved working with Stevie. He was different from the boys at school: for one thing, he hadn't liked her right away. In fact, he had clearly *dis*liked her. But she had earned his respect and he had earned hers. Stevie was the first boy who had really treated her just as a person, who had fought with her, disagreed with her. And usually, working with him made her feel safe—she knew he had her back. Now, though, even with the people she felt closest to, she was uncomfortable.

She liked the idea of breaking a story and the fact that she could get people to talk to her. But she wondered where the line was where you crossed over from reporting to being some kind of investigator she had never set out to be.

Pete Dowling and Bob Campbell were sitting on a bench at the corner of the seawall. There was a light right behind the bench and, reading the inscription, Susan Carol learned the light had originally been on a ship called the *Triton*.

"I'll say one thing for you guys, you know how to pick a pretty spot," Kelleher said.

"Didn't even notice, to be honest," Dowling said. "I just wanted to get far enough away from the practice field that no one would see us."

"So what's up?" Kelleher said, leaning against the sea-wall.

Dowling look at Campbell and then responded in carefully chosen words. "We know you're thinking that we might have some concerns about the Arnott family." He stopped for a moment. "I'm willing to fill you in on what's going on, but it has to be off the record."

"Why?" Kelleher asked.

"What do you mean why?" Dowling asked.

"Well, yesterday afternoon, you let me know, in no

uncertain terms, that you wanted Stevie and Susan Carol to back off. Now you want to fill us in, but it has to be off the record. Why?"

Both Bobby and Tamara had always counseled them that you never let someone go off the record without at least explaining why first. At the very least it made the person feel a little beholden to you for cooperating.

"We're willing to talk because we think you're likely to make the situation worse if you don't know what's going on. And we need to go off the record because if you print any of this, it could jeopardize an ongoing FBI operation."

That news was shocking enough to silence everyone for a moment. Kelleher regained his composure first.

"As long as that's really the case, then I'm okay with off the record," Kelleher said.

"Come on, Bobby, we've known each other a long time," Dowling said. "Have I ever misled you?"

"No. I don't think you have. Okay, let's hear it."

Dowling turned to Campbell. "Go ahead, Bob, you're the one who knows it best."

"Okay. The FBI has an agent inside a white supremacy group called the Knights of the White Christian Soldiers—it's something like the KKK, but nowhere near as well organized. And one of the members of that group is Michael Arnott—father to both Michael Junior and Alan.

"And last night, the FBI alerted us that Mr. Arnott had been talking about the Army-Navy game at a specially called meeting."

"Whoa," Stevie couldn't help saying.

Susan Carol's heart sank a little—she'd really liked Michael Arnott. Clearly his differences with his father were more serious than he'd let on.

"He said he believed his sons had been singled out by us for special attention. He said we'd interviewed a lot of kids for background but thought his sons were really our targets."

"What made him think that?" Stevie asked.

"Could just be paranoia." Campbell shrugged. "But the point is that he seemed to the FBI agent to be inordinately upset about it. He could just be pissed off that his sons are being questioned. Or it could be that our attention is messing up some plan of his."

"But," Stevie couldn't help interjecting again, "did they talk about a plan?"

Campbell shook his head. "Nothing specific, no," he said. "But there was enough talk about the Army-Navy game and the fact that the president was going to be there to make the FBI alert us."

"Does this group have any history of violence?" Tamara asked.

"Nothing that's been proven so far. But if the FBI feels it's worth having a man inside, we have to believe it's a possibility."

That pronouncement made for another sobering pause in the conversation.

Then Dowling continued. "So, Susan Carol. We know you're slated to talk to Alan Arnott. And I'm asking you *not* to dig into his family."

"But the whole point of the interview is to talk about his brother at Army," she said.

"Right—his brother is fine. Just stay away from the father and politics and the president."

"But I've been asking *everyone* about those things—what it means to have the president at the game, things like that. Wouldn't it be more suspicious *not* to ask?" Susan Carol said. She wasn't sure why she was arguing, really. She just hated the whole situation.

Dowling sighed. "Look, Susan Carol, I'm going to ask you to use your best judgment.

"I need you all to take this seriously. The FBI agent feels that the other members of the KWCS are suspicious of him. So if you push too hard, or ask questions about white supremacy groups, or seem to know too much, it could come back on him, and that's the last thing we need right now."

"But I *don't* know much," Susan Carol protested.

"No." Dowling gave the barest hint of a smile. "But you've proven yourself to be a good guesser."

The reporters walked back to the practice field in silence.

The postpractice plan was still the same, but suddenly everything felt different.

OFFICIAL INQUIRIES

Once the players had broken their huddle at the end of practice, Stevie saw Scott Strasemeier walking in his direction with Ricky Dobbs, who was wearing the red practice jersey that quarterbacks wore to let defenders know they weren't supposed to be hit.

"Steve, this is Ricky Dobbs," Strasemeier said. "We're going to do a couple of TV interviews here on the field, and then it will be just you and Christian Swezey from GoMids.com inside."

Stevie shook hands with Dobbs, who said, "Steve, we met at lunch in Philadelphia—good to see you again." Stevie remembered reading that Dobbs said he might want to run for president someday. And watching him now, with his light-up-the-world smile, made Stevie think it was possible.

While Dobbs talked to Bret Haber and his crew from

Channel 9, Stevie stood a few yards away watching. When Haber asked about the officiating at Notre Dame, Dobbs had his answer ready.

"We've already forgotten about that," he said. "You can't dwell on the past; it doesn't do any good. Plus, we still had chances to win the game and we just didn't get it done."

Perfect answer, Stevie thought, except he didn't believe it for a minute. He remembered Eddie Brennan, the quarterback of the California Dreams, telling him that he remembered every single bad call that had ever been made against one of his teams. "That includes peewee football when I was eight," he said.

Stevie was making a mental note to ask Dobbs how he *really* felt about the officiating when Christian Swezey walked up and introduced himself. He was tall and had blond curly hair and a friendly smile.

"I just wanted to tell you that I think it's really awesome that we're going to interview Dobbs together," Swezey said. "I just can't believe the stories you've broken and written. You and Susan Carol are absolutely *amazing*."

"Well, thanks," Stevie said, liking Swezey right away for obvious reasons.

Dobbs finished his last TV interview—telling Russ Thaler, who worked for the DC-based outlet of Comcast SportsNet, that playing in the Army-Navy game was "an honor for everyone who puts on the uniform."

That comment Stevie believed.

Once the TV people were done, Strasemeier got them settled in a small conference room. If there was a time limit, he didn't say anything about it. Dobbs obviously knew Swezey.

"How's our lacrosse team going to be, Christian?" he asked, then said to Stevie, "Christian is the man when it comes to lacrosse."

"He's exaggerating," Swezey said. "I just cover it a little bit."

He then launched into a five-minute breakdown of the Navy lacrosse team position by position that left Stevie feeling a bit dazed. When he paused for breath, Stevie jumped in and said, "Okay, no cameras rolling here, how did you *really* feel about the officiating at Notre Dame?"

Dobbs looked him right in the eye. "You quoting me?"

"Not if you don't want me to," Stevie said. "I'd just like to know what the players really thought."

"Not to be quoted, they should put those guys in jail," Dobbs said. "I mean, if stealing is a crime . . ."

That was all Stevie needed to hear. He was testing his theory more than looking for a story. For the next twenty minutes, they talked about life at Navy, Dobbs's winning a dance contest the previous year, and his political ambitions.

"I met President Obama when we went to the White House after winning the Commander-in-Chief's Trophy last year," Dobbs said. "But it'll be great to have him at that game, and he's going to come in the locker room to meet the team with no cameras or anything. That's what I'm most looking forward to."

"Does all the extra security with the president coming bother you at all?" Stevie asked.

Dobbs shook his head. "No, not at all. We're used to security around here. We understand why they have to do it. I've heard a couple of guys complain, but they're guys who voted for Senator McCain."

"McCain did graduate from Navy," Swezey said.

"Yes. And he's a good man," Dobbs said. "I've met him too. He's a hero. But a few of our guys, to tell you the truth, I think have some trouble with an African American being president."

That comment surprised Stevie.

"Really?" he said. "Didn't you get voted team captain this year?"

Dobbs laughed. "Captain of the Navy football team is a little different than president of the United States, isn't it? Plus, I'm not talking about most of the guys or even some of the guys, I'm talking about a small handful. It's not a big deal. Arguing politics is a sport of its own here. I enjoy disagreeing with those guys."

"Even when it's racial?" Swezey said.

"Racial arguments are nothing new for me," Dobbs said. "I'm from Georgia. Some guys here grew up in all-white environments and they're just learning that they don't live in an all-white world. They'll come around. I will tell you this, though: you can't be an African American in this country and not encounter racism."

He paused for a moment and said, "Don't quote me on this because I don't want to make it a bigger deal than it is, but when we've been on the road, I've had fans say things to me as we're coming out of the tunnel. I even had a ref say something."

"A REF?" Stevie and Swezey both said.

"Yeah. I was arguing a call with a guy—he'd called a chop block, and I was asking him how he could call it when there was only one guy involved and there have to be two for a chop block.

"He looked at me and said, 'Son, only your captain can talk to the officials.' I said, 'I AM the captain,' and he said, 'I don't believe it,' and walked away."

"And you thought that he said that because you're black?" Stevie asked.

"I know he said it because I'm black," Dobbs said. "I've heard that tone enough times in my life to recognize it. Hey, how did we get on this subject?"

"President Obama," Stevie said.

"Right, I forgot. Bottom line, and I mean this: I think everyone is very psyched about him being there."

"Everybody?" Stevie asked.

"Yes," he said. "Everybody."

They broke up a few minutes later. Stevie walked back outside and found Tamara and Susan Carol waiting for him.

"Where's Bobby?" he asked.

"Still with Kenny," Tamara said. "He had to wait

because Kenny had to do all his TV stuff. They've been talking a while, though, so I hope he's getting something."

"How'd you guys do?" Stevie asked.

"I talked to Chet," she said. "He said the Secret Service explained they're going to ratchet up security as a precaution, but as of right now, there's nothing that will affect what they're doing this week."

"And you?" Stevie said, looking at Susan Carol, who seemed subdued.

She sighed. "Just like his brother, Alan Arnott is a smart, good kid. I've got a really good feature story on the two brothers but no new information. I wonder if the brothers even know about their father being in that group. It's really hard to imagine, having met them."

Stevie filled them in on what Dobbs had said about encountering racism during a game. "Interesting stuff," Tamara said. "But I don't think it carries the story any farther."

"No, but I'd sure like to meet that ref," Stevie said. "I just can't believe it. And the fans—how do you go to a football game and yell something at a player from *Navy?*"

"I'm not so shocked," Susan Carol said. "I hear stuff like that all time where I live. Mostly from older people—not so much with kids my age. But still. It's out there."

Kelleher was walking in their direction with Niumatalolo. "So I hear you had great weather at Army yesterday," Niumatalolo said as he shook hands with everyone.

"Just remember we made arrangements for perfect weather for you here at Navy."

They all laughed, happy to have the mood lightened a bit.

"Sorry I have to run," Niumatalolo said. "I have to get inside and meet with my coaches."

"You'll stay in touch, right?" Kelleher said.

"You have my word," Niumatalolo said.

He waved to everyone and walked off.

"Get anything?" Tamara said.

"Yeah," Kelleher said. "I'll tell you about it in the car. We need to get back to the office so we can all write."

As they were driving out the gate, Kelleher filled them in.

"Obviously we can't use this right now for about a million reasons," he said. "But Kenny said the Secret Service told him that they may not let the Arnott family into the game."

"They can do that?" Susan Carol said.

"They can keep anyone they want out of the game if they believe their presence might be a danger to the president," Kelleher said.

"Do you think the president is in any real danger?" Susan Carol asked.

"I don't," Kelleher said. "If there's something going on—and that still seems like a big *if* to me—the FBI and the Secret Service are on it and they know what they're doing. I *do* think getting into that stadium next Saturday is going to be a real nightmare."

"So we keep after the story, then?" Stevie asked.

"Oh yeah," Bobby said. "We're like the Secret Service. We don't take anything for granted and we don't assume anything. Hey, there's one other thing Kenny told me that may be just as interesting on another front."

"What's that?" Tamara asked.

"They tried to get the officiating crew changed. Kenny and Chet said they didn't want anyone who was on the Notre Dame crew on the game."

"How'd that go over?" Susan Carol asked, instantly intrigued.

"Not well. In fact, they're still fighting about it. The ACC, which assigns the officials, said it wouldn't change the crew, there was no reason to change the crew, and they were insulted by the request. Kenny responded by sending the tape of the two plays from Notre Dame with a note that said, 'You show me where there was a hold on either play and I'll shut up. Otherwise, I want different officials.'"

"And?" Susan Carol asked.

"They sent the tape Friday. They haven't heard anything back."

"What a surprise," Susan Carol said bitterly. "The refs are all too busy writing letters to the editor."

Back at the *Post,* as they were coming off the elevators, they ran into Bob Woodward.

"Hey, it's the four Musketeers," Woodward said. "Have you guys been able to keep Bobby in line this week?"

"Almost. Actually, it's these two we've had trouble with—as usual," Tamara said, pointing to Stevie and Susan Carol.

"Oh yes, this must be the famous Susan Carol," Woodward said, putting his hand out. "I'm Bob Woodward. Great piece on the Notre Dame–Navy game. I'm with you on the referees. I say never trust them."

In all the time he had known her, Stevie had never seen Susan Carol anywhere close to speechless. Now she could barely stammer back, "It's an honor to meet you, Mr. Woodward."

"Bob," Woodward said. "Where are you from, Susan Carol? Obviously somewhere in the South."

"I'm from . . ." Susan Carol paused. "I'm from . . ." She stopped again. Stevie was amazed. He'd seen her cool, calm, and collected while talking to Matt Damon, to star quarterback Eddie Brennan, to any number of famous people. Now she was completely flustered.

"Goldsboro, North Carolina," Tamara said, coming to the rescue.

"I'm from a small town too," Woodward said, patting her on the shoulder. "Wheaton, Illinois. It's very nice to meet you. You guys keep up the good work."

An elevator had arrived and he stepped onto it with a wave goodbye.

Stevie looked at Susan Carol. All color had drained from her face. "I—I can't believe it," she stammered. "I forgot where I was from."

"Bob is so un-intimidating he can be intimidating," Tamara said. "Don't worry about it."

"Don't worry about it? I just met Bob Woodward and I couldn't remember where I *lived*. I've never been so humiliated in my life!"

"Trust me, Bob will judge you only by what you write," Kelleher said. "Speaking of which, let's get going."

Stevie had a lot of one-liners running through his head as they walked back to sports, but he resisted. He'd save them for when he really needed them. . . .

As was often the case, Stevie's biggest problem in writing about the two quarterbacks, Ricky Dobbs and Trent Steelman, was deciding what to leave out. He had enough to write two thousand words easily.

"Write two thousand if you want," Kelleher said. "They'll just use the best one thousand."

"I'm betting that line isn't original," Stevie said. "It sounds like something an editor would say."

"George Minot," Kelleher said. "One of my first editors right out of college. That was always his line when I asked for extra space. He meant it too."

Susan Carol was given fifteen hundred words to write about the Arnott brothers and how one had ended up at Army, the other at Navy, and what it would be like for the two of them to play against each other in the biggest game of their lives.

Stevie finished first and read some of Susan Carol's story over her shoulder.

In a perfect world, Michael and Alan Arnott would run out of the same tunnel this coming Saturday, wearing the same uniform, ready to do what they did throughout their boyhood: work together to win a football game. But life is never that simple, especially when it comes to college football. Neither Arnott was recruited by any of the major football-playing schools, but Navy defensive coordinator Buddy Green thought Alan Arnott had the potential to play linebacker for his team.

"He was like a lot of players who have had success for us in the past," Green said. "He wasn't that big [5-11, 195 pounds] or that fast. But he had the ability to find his way to the football. Some of our best linebackers have been exactly like Alan."

Green's instincts proved correct. Arnott broke into the starting lineup as a sophomore, and this year, as a junior, he is second in tackles and has three interceptions and four sacks. The only thing missing in his Navy experience is the presence of Michael, his younger brother. "Once I came here, I hoped Mike would follow me," he said. "We've always been close. But he's a tight end and there's no tight end in our offense. Army offered him his best chance to play."

Michael Arnott is now Army's starting tight end. This coming Saturday, when Army and Navy play for the 110th time, chances are good that the Arnott brothers will come face to face, or more accurately face mask to face mask, with one another.

Stevie stopped reading. "That's really good," he said.

"They're both good talkers," Susan Carol said. "Makes it easy."

"Being good makes it easy," Stevie said. "Don't let one dumb letter make you think any different."

That earned him a kiss. Which pretty much made his day.

GAME DAY: 18 MINUTES TO KICKOFF

Stevie heard a loud cheer coming from the Navy side of the field. The stadium, which seated more than ninety-two thousand, was now filled to capacity. The Midshipmen, led by Ricky Dobbs and Wyatt Middleton, had appeared in their tunnel, wearing their white uniforms and gold helmets. A TV functionary wearing a headset stood in front of the remaining players, obviously waiting for the signal to send Navy onto the field.

When it finally came, the players streamed from the tunnel. Two players carried American flags, and five cheerleaders streaked across the field carrying massive flags that said N, A, V, Y and GO MIDS! The crowd on the Navy side went crazy. Stevie noticed Dobbs and Middleton, escorted by cops and at least one Secret Service agent, break away to head for midfield.

As soon as the Navy players had begun their sprint, the Army players raced onto the field from the opposite tunnel, and now the explosion of applause came from behind where Stevie and Susan Carol were standing at the 25-yard line.

Both bands were playing their fight songs. The place was impossibly loud.

But then it got louder still. Six F-15E Strike Eagles flew in formation low over the field. The sleek gray jets were gone almost as soon as Stevie noticed them. But the sound of them came a couple seconds later, and Stevie could feel it vibrating up through his feet and rattling in his chest. That drowned out even the crowd noise for a minute.

Everything seemed to be happening fast now.

Tim Kelly, Dick Hall, and Dean Taylor were jogging down the sideline, having followed the Army team onto the field. They spotted Stevie and Susan Carol and waved.

Secret Service agents were also pouring out of the tunnel and fanning out around the field.

"Stay close to us now," Dowling said. "You wander off somewhere, you're apt to be taken off the field by an agent who doesn't know you."

"Even with all-access passes?" Stevie said.

Dowling laughed. "They mean nothing once the president walks in here," he said. "*I'm* your all-access pass right now."

Even though he'd laughed briefly, Susan Carol could sense the tension in his voice. The president was about to arrive on field. This had to be the scariest time for the agents.

Then the Army band started to play "Hail to the Chief," and everyone turned to face the Army tunnel. And suddenly, there he was—the president—looking just as relaxed and happy as he had when she'd met him in his office last Monday.

THE WHITE HOUSE

Stevie was dressed up in a blue blazer and gray pants and a carefully knotted tie, but he gawked when Susan Carol came downstairs in a tailored blue dress and high heels.

"Heels?" Stevie said.

"I'm goin' to the White House to meet the president of the United States," she said. "Should I be wearin' sneakers?"

"No," he said. "But it isn't a state dinner, it's an interview."

"Lay off, Stevie," said Kelleher, who was standing at the stove making eggs. "She looks great and so do you. Just make sure you both remember a tape recorder *and* a notebook. They'll probably have someone there taping the interview too, but it's always good to have backup."

Stevie had been pretty calm about the interview—right to the moment they pulled up at the White House gate.

Bob Campbell was waiting outside for them.

"Right on time," he said, looking at his watch.

"I don't imagine too many people are late for appointments with the president," Susan Carol said.

"True," Campbell said. "Most of the time it's the other way around. President Obama is actually pretty good as presidents go about staying on time."

"Anyone who was really bad?" Stevie asked.

"President Clinton." Campbell laughed. "On a good day he was two hours behind schedule. Come on, let's get you through security and I'll give you a ten-minute tour."

The security check was thorough but not too bad. They had already been given clearance since their social security numbers had been submitted a couple of weeks earlier. The guards were friendly, no doubt in part because of Campbell's presence. Once they were inside the gate, they walked through a small parking lot that sat between the White House and a massive older-looking building that was connected to the White House with a canopy.

"What's that building?" Stevie asked, hearing Susan Carol sigh loudly as soon as the question was out of his mouth.

"That's the OEOB," Dowling said.

"The OEO what?" Stevie said.

Susan Carol was now rolling her eyes. "Steven Thomas, have you never even watched *West Wing?*" she said. "The OEOB is the Old Executive Office Building. It's where most of the White House staff works."

"I have watched *West Wing,*" Stevie said. "I just didn't

memorize it. So the White House staff all works over there?"

"Most of it, actually," Campbell said. "Only those who need to be closest to the president actually work in the White House itself."

They walked into a small lobby filled with photos of President Obama with various people, most of whom Stevie didn't recognize. One he did recognize was Ken Niumatalolo, standing next to the president, who was holding up a Navy football jersey with his name and a number 1 on it. Seeing him staring at the photo, Campbell pointed at it.

"That's the only one up there now that wasn't taken in the last month," he said. "Most of the photos put up here are recent. But for Army-Navy week they dug that one out. It's from last April when the Navy team came here to officially receive the Commander-in-Chief's Trophy."

"So the winner of the game gets to come to the White House," Stevie said.

"The winner of the *trophy* does," Campbell said. "Since Army and Navy both beat Air Force this year, yes, the winner Saturday will be coming here at some point."

They continued down a hall and Campbell stopped at a door with a guard on it. "Hey, Mike, I just want to give the kids a quick look if nothing's going on," he said.

"All quiet," Mike said, hitting some kind of button on the wall that swung the door open. They walked into a small room with a long table in the middle, clocks on one of the walls, and what looked like a computer screen of some kind on the far wall.

"Know what this is?"

"The situation room, right?" Susan Carol said.

"No way," Stevie said. "It can't be this small."

"That's what most people say. But you're right, Susan Carol. Come on, we'll go upstairs and I'll show you the press room. You'll be surprised at how small it is too."

They went up a flight of stairs, down a couple of very busy hallways, and through a door into an interview room that was about half the size of the interview room Stevie had been in at West Point a week earlier and maybe one-tenth the size of an interview room at the Final Four or the Super Bowl.

"The White House press room," Campbell said.

The only reason Stevie believed him was that he could see a podium with the presidential seal and a White House logo behind it. It appeared to seat fewer than a hundred.

"Come on, it's almost ten," Campbell said, walking them back down the hall and into a large office that had three desks and about a dozen people, all seeming busy.

"This is Reggie Love. You guys may have heard or read about him. . . ."

"You played at Duke!" Susan Carol practically shrieked as Love stood up to greet them. "I've read all about you!"

"And I've read about both of you," Love said, smiling. He was huge, at least six foot six, and built like a football player.

"Reggie started playing football at Duke," Susan Carol was explaining. "But in 2001, Coach K. asked him to join the basketball team because they needed depth inside, and he played on the national championship team that year."

Reggie Love held up his left hand. "Yup, I still wear my championship ring," he said. "It's nice to meet you both. The president's nine o'clock is wrapping up right now."

Almost on cue, a door behind Love opened and a half dozen people poured out. Stevie recognized one of them instantly. "Hillary Clinton," Susan Carol hissed as the secretary of state gave them a smile walking by.

"*That* I know," Stevie said.

"Come on in," Love said, walking to the door. Campbell, Stevie noticed, had not followed them.

"Mr. President," Love said. "Susan Carol Anderson and Steve Thomas."

At first, Stevie only heard the familiar voice.

"Thanks, Reggie," he heard him say. Then, as Love stepped back to let him and Susan Carol walk inside the Oval Office, the president of the United States walked around his desk to come and greet them.

"Steve, Susan Carol, this is a real pleasure," he said, shaking hands. "I'm Barack Obama."

A photographer took several pictures of Stevie and Susan Carol sitting on the couch, notebooks poised, while the president sat in an armchair.

"We'll send you copies," he said.

"Do you need our addresses?" Stevie asked.

The president laughed at that one. "We have your addresses, Steve," he said.

Oh yeah, Stevie thought. They have everyone's address.

Stevie and Susan Carol started the interview with softball questions about Army-Navy and what connections the president had to the rivalry.

"I'm a fan," he said. "I can remember watching the game one year when a Navy kid missed a short field goal at the end in a driving rain to lose the game and then took all the blame on himself, didn't make any excuses. I was impressed by that."

"Ryan Bucchianeri was his name," Susan Carol said. It figured, Stevie thought, she would know that.

"That's it, I remember him," the president said. "Then there was a game where Army drove, I think, ninety-nine yards to win.

"Of course now the game means even more to me. As commander in chief, I have a connection to these young men that goes beyond being a football fan."

They continued in a jock vein for a while. President Obama either was a real fan or had been briefed well. He certainly knew all about Stevie and Susan Carol. At one point he asked Susan Carol what her current national ranking was in the 100 butterfly.

"I'm actually a little higher in the 200," she said. "I'm fourth right now."

"The 200 'fly?" the president said. "I get tired just watching that event."

Susan Carol smiled, clearly delighted that the president could talk swimming. "The last time I swam it, I died completely at the finish."

"You'll get 'em next time," the president said.

It was Susan Carol who finally brought up security at the game. Pete Dowling had told Kelleher that the president was always briefed on security issues, but they weren't sure if he knew *they* knew.

"Are you concerned about it at all?" Susan Carol asked.

"No—I have the Secret Service to be concerned about it for me," he said. "When you're president, there are always going to be people who have some kind of grudge against you. It comes with the territory."

"More so when you are an African American president?" Stevie asked, proud that his voice wasn't trembling.

"I've been an African American president since the day I was sworn in," the president said, smiling. "Again, that's just part of who I am. I know that adds some new stresses for the Secret Service, but I also know just how good they are at their jobs. I don't look over my shoulder. Lots of professionals are there to protect me."

Stevie knew they were out of time. Reggie Love poked his head in the door. "Mr. President?" he said. "It's ten twenty-five. Your ten fifteen is waiting outside." They had been scheduled to have fifteen minutes. They'd been given twenty-five.

The president stood up. "I know you two understand that the security questions have to be off the record at least until after the game. Pete told me you'd had that conversation."

They both nodded. Stevie wasn't about to explain to the president of the United States that technically he should have gone off the record before answering the questions.

Then the president laughed. "And also off the record? I think the officials have more to worry about from you, Ms. Anderson. People will be paying more attention to them than to me, I suspect."

Susan Carol blushed fiercely, so Stevie thanked him again and they were escorted out.

As they were leaving, Stevie couldn't help but notice the president's 10:15 standing up to be escorted into the Oval Office.

It was Bill Gates.

BEST PRACTICES

Once Campbell had escorted them back to the northwest gate, they walked to the *Post*. They were told to "just write" and not worry about length, and that's what they did—producing two thousand words in under two hours.

"He really is good," Kelleher said, reading behind them. "He knows exactly what people need and he gives it to them—nothing more, nothing less."

Once their story had been edited and approved, Kelleher took Stevie to the train station. He was dreading the next few days: he'd be back in school, which was a pretty big comedown from interviewing the president. But soon he'd be at the game itself. Just not soon enough.

Susan Carol was happy with the story she and Stevie had produced from their interview with President Obama.

And she liked having people stop her in the newsroom to tell her how much they had enjoyed her story on the Arnott brothers in that morning's paper. Tamara called it "taking bows."

"No better feeling," she said. "It's great to write something your colleagues notice."

"Well, it sure beats hate mail." Susan Carol laughed.

She also felt better after a weekend working together with Stevie. Even tough things seemed better when they could tackle them together.

So she really missed Stevie when Kelleher called her on Tuesday.

"I just got a call from Kenny Niumatalolo," he said. "He told me the ACC stuck to its guns on the refs, so your favorite officials from the Notre Dame game will be on the Army-Navy game. He's really angry about it."

"Are you going to write about it?" she asked.

"No. You are. You were the one who started this story."

Susan Carol was quiet, so Kelleher plowed ahead. "Don't be nervous. You just make some phone calls. I'll give you Kenny's cell. I think he'll talk pretty frankly even on the record because he is *not* happy. Then call the ACC for comment, and Rich Ellerson too. You've got his number, right?"

"What about the referee; do I call him too?" she asked.

"Ask Harold Neve—he's the ACC's football supervisor— if he's got numbers for any of the four guys. They all have jobs, so they're probably reachable at their offices."

"They have jobs?"

"Sure. They only ref one day a week, travel one day maybe, and football season is only so long. So the rest of the time they have jobs. That's part of the problem, really. They're not full-time professionals and no one ever wants to fire them when they screw up."

Susan Carol wasn't terribly excited about doing the story, but she knew it needed to be done.

Niumatalolo was calm but clearly upset when she talked to him.

"I have yet to see any evidence that those two calls were warranted," he said. "I really don't think it's fair to our kids to run onto the field for our biggest game of the year and have to see four of those same officials out there. I'm not saying they're incompetent, I'm just saying the wound they inflicted is still raw."

Ellerson was sympathetic with Niumatalolo. "If I was in Ken's shoes, I'd probably feel the same way," he said. "My only concern now is that the officials might *not* want to makes calls against Navy. Honestly, I'd rather not see them on the game either."

Not surprisingly, the ACC football supervisor, Harold Neve, wasn't at all pleased when Susan Carol read him the coaches' comments. "Mike Daniels has been officiating for twenty-two years. He's been a referee for fourteen. All the men involved are very experienced and have excellent records. They're looking forward to this game—being a part of it is special for the officials too.

"It's not unusual for a coach to be upset about a couple of calls. But we don't change assignments because of it."

"Did you look at the game tape?" Susan Carol asked.

"Of course I did," Neve said.

"And?"

"And I don't comment on specific plays except to explain a rule. These were judgment calls. I don't talk about judgment calls. But if I thought any official in any game had badly blown a call, you can be sure he would hear about it from me."

"Did the officials in the Navy–Notre Dame game hear from you?"

Neve didn't answer the question. "You know, young lady, a lot of this happened because of the inflammatory story you wrote. So I really don't appreciate your attitude."

Now Susan Carol was angry. "I think I gave people a pretty clear picture of what happened."

"You focused on two calls. How many other calls made up that game? How many plays went off with no call necessary?"

"But those two calls both came at key moments—" Susan Carol cut herself off. She realized she was arguing, not interviewing, a cardinal sin for a reporter. Before Neve could respond, she said, "Look, Mr. Neve, thanks for your help. Do you have phone numbers where I might reach the four officials?"

There was silence on the other end for a moment.

"Our policy is to only allow referees to speak to the media, and only if they choose to do so," he said. "The referee is the spokesman. I'll give you Mike Daniels's number if you want it, but I doubt he'll want to talk to you."

"I know that," she said. "But I think I should give him a chance to comment."

"Fine, then."

He gave her the number. Hanging up the phone, Susan Carol felt a wave of resolve come over her. So without hesitating, she called the number he had given her.

"G. A. Storage Company, may I help you?" a voice said.

"I was trying to reach Mike Daniels."

There was clearly no call-screening at G. A. Storage Company because she was put right through. On the second ring someone picked up and said, "Mike Daniels."

For a split second, Susan Carol froze. Then she found her voice.

"Mr. Daniels, this is Susan Carol Anderson from the *Washington Post*."

Silence.

"Mr. Daniels?"

"What can you possibly want?"

"I'm writing a story about the fact that Coach Ken Niumatalolo asked that you and your crew mates be removed from the Army-Navy game." She was talking fast, hoping he wouldn't hang up on her. "I talked to Mr. Neve, and he gave me your number."

"He did?"

"He said you were the spokesman for the crew. And that it would be up to you to comment."

"Okay, here's my comment: the fact that we're still assigned to the game is proof of the job we've done this year. If Coach Niumatalolo has a problem with that, it's his problem. Not ours."

"But don't you think—"

She stopped. The phone had gone dead. Which, in truth, was fine with her. If Daniels hadn't been hostile, she would have been surprised—and maybe even a little disappointed. She turned to the computer and started to write.

On Wednesday, Susan Carol and Tamara were back at Navy for practice.

"Tomorrow is our last real practice before Saturday," Coach Niumatalolo said as the players gathered around at the end of their workout. It was six o'clock, pitch dark, and cold. No one seemed to notice. "We're going to have to go straight from practice to the pep rally on T-Court and we'll be pressed for time, so I'd like the captains to talk to you right now."

"What's T-Court?" Susan Carol whispered to Tamara as Ricky Dobbs stood up in front of his teammates.

"Tecumseh Court," she answered. "There's a statue of the Indian Tecumseh on a green. Everyone calls it T-Court."

Dobbs spoke softly. "We seniors have talked about the fact that this is our last Army-Navy game," he said. "So I want to talk to you underclassmen. Your time is going to come for this. You're going to remember your last practice on this field, your last time dressing in the locker room, the last time you run on the field to play against Army, the last time you stand for the alma maters after we get through kicking their butts."

That got a little cheer from everyone.

"Seriously, though, I know from talking to guys who were here long before us that no matter what the outcome on Saturday, this is the game we'll remember most. It's great we've whipped Air Force every year. But we all know the first thing we're going to talk about at our reunions is playing Army. The first thing any of us will be asked when we report for active duty will be, 'What was your record against Army?' The last five senior classes all got to say, four and oh. I want to be able to say the same, and so do all of you."

He sat down to raucous applause.

Defensive back Wyatt Middleton, the defensive captain, was next. He repeated a lot of the things Dobbs had said, but he finished on a different note. "I read a quote about this game from an Army coach named Bob Sutton," he said. "Bob Sutton beat us six out of nine when he was the coach. He said he always told his team, 'Think about how much you want to win this game. Think about what it will mean to you the rest of your life. Then think about this: the Navy guys feel exactly the same way.'"

Middleton paused. "He also said this: 'The most desperate team wins the Army-Navy game.' So think. We've beaten these guys eight years in a row. Can you imagine how desperate they are? We know they're good this year. And I know that we are better. But we also have to find a way to be more *desperate* on Saturday. That's what's going to make the difference."

When he finished, the entire team stood and formed a circle around the captains. "On three," Middleton said. "One, two, three . . . BE DESPERATE!"

Then the team fell into handshakes and embraces with the two captains.

"Wow," Susan Carol said.

"You said it," Tamara said.

Two hundred miles north, Stevie was at West Point for one of Army's last practices. It was the last day of full hitting. Thursday would be devoted to making sure they knew Navy's schemes and to special teams. By 6:30 the sun was down and it was getting very cold, and Rich Ellerson blew his whistle and called everyone to the middle of the field.

"Get ready for this," Tim Kelly leaned in and said quietly to Stevie.

Stevie was prepared for a speech.

"There are twenty-four first classmen on this football team," Ellerson said. "To say that every one of them is a special person sounds like a cliché, but we all know what it takes to play four years of football here. I wasn't here for their first year, but I'm told that at the first practice that August, one hundred and eight plebes reported to play football. These are the guys who stuck it out."

One by one he called each senior to stand next to him.

As each player came up, Ellerson talked about him—told a funny story, talked about a big play he had made, quoted something one of his teammates had said about him. There were lots of laughs, a few tears, and a lot of applause for each player. Ellerson didn't call the players up in order of importance or based on whether they were starters; he brought them up alphabetically.

The last senior was Jim Zopelis, a special teams player. Stevie knew Zopelis was famous for his imitations, and the one he enjoyed doing most was of Doug Pavek, one of the officer reps who had been a cornerback twenty-five years earlier at Army. Pavek liked to give pep talks to the team, and apparently he always began them by saying, "Guys, I played in TWO bowl games while I was a player at Army . . . TWO bowl games."

Ellerson asked Zopelis to do Pavek for everyone one more time.

"Coach, so far I've played in NO bowl games," Zopelis riffed. "None, zero, not one. But by God, I'm going to win ONE game against Navy before I go. ONE GAME!"

The whole team roared their approval.

Ellerson said, "Okay, guys, let's line up."

Then everyone except for Stevie and Dean Taylor, the former team doctor (who was visiting for the week but technically a visitor too), and the twenty-four seniors walked to the far end zone, where the players entered the field for games. They formed a cordon—players, coaches, trainers, doctors, everyone. Once they were lined up, the first classmen, one by one, made their way along the cordon. There were handshakes and hugs for each as they passed through their teammates. When the last of them—Zopelis—had shaken the last hand—Ellerson's—the coach and everyone else simply turned to the seniors and applauded.

Stevie's story poured out:

There are many traditions that make up the Army-Navy experience. Most will be carried out on Saturday in front of more than 90,000 witnesses inside FedEx Field. But Wednesday night, under an almost-full moon, one of football's most emotional traditions took place inside an empty Michie Stadium while a cold wind whistled in off the Hudson.

After each of Army's 24 seniors, surrounded by their teammates, had been called up by Coach Rich Ellerson for a final salute to their careers, the coaches and staff members and underclassmen formed a cordon leading from the field to the locker room.

Slowly, clearly savoring every moment, every handshake, every hug, the 24 seniors walked through the cordon to say goodbye—not just to their coaches and teammates, but also to the long practice days inside this old stadium filled with memories and banners honoring past national champions and Heisman Trophy winners.

And after the last senior had hugged Ellerson, the man standing at the end of the cordon, the first classmen stood before their team and received a heartfelt round of applause that echoed off the stadium's empty seats.

It was a moment of bonding and camaraderie and, yes, love. All 24 seniors have loved playing football for Army. And everyone inside Michie Stadium this evening loved being part of their achievement.

Stevie leaned back in his chair. He wondered if what he had written was too corny. But Kelleher had once told him that nothing was too corny if it was true. So he pressed send and filed the story.

PARTY DUTY

"**W**elcome back," said Tamara when Stevie arrived at the *Post* offices on Friday afternoon. He felt like he'd worn a path up and down the East Coast the past few weeks, from West Point to Philly to DC to Annapolis—he was glad to be on his last trip. This was it. Army-Navy game weekend—at last.

"Susan Carol is upstairs writing. And Bobby went over to see Pete Dowling. He should be back soon."

As they rode the elevator up to the fifth floor, Stevie asked if the meeting with Dowling was just a routine update or if something new was up.

"I'm not sure," Tamara answered. "But Pete called Bobby."

Stevie was still pondering that when they reached the sports department and Susan Carol, dressed in jeans and (hallelujah) sneakers, ran up to give him a hug. "I saved some extra copies of the paper for you," she said.

Stevie looked at the sports section she was putting in his hands and there were their stories, side by side at the top of the page. There was one headline for both of them that said: FAREWELLS IN ARMS. A photo underneath showed Ricky Dobbs being hugged by two of his teammates.

There was yet another meeting to discuss plans for game-day coverage. Stevie and Susan Carol, in addition to working with Kelleher and Mearns on the security story, had what Matt Vita called "party duty." There was an official party that night at the convention center. If there was any news, they'd file a story for the Sunday paper on what was called "the scene." Stevie was jaded enough to roll his eyes at that one.

"What's the matter with you?" Susan Carol hissed in his ear.

"Party reporting is for girls," Stevie whispered back.

"There will probably be *lots* of food," Susan Carol said, after kicking him under the table. "And you'll be my date. Does that sound so bad?"

Actually, it sounded pretty good. Stevie decided to shut up.

The convention center party was enormous. There were banners and bunting, and everything was decked out in Navy blue and gold and Army black and gold. Stevie had never seen so many people in military uniforms in his life. Kelleher pointed out a few big boosters. Apparently even Army and Navy had boosters.

"They need boosters," Kelleher explained. "Their athletic departments aren't government-funded. They're private nonprofit entities. Basically, they have to make enough money off football and from donations to fund all their other sports."

They pushed their way into the party, meeting and greeting as they went. Everywhere Stevie turned, another celebrity bobbed into his line of vision: Gary Williams, the Maryland basketball coach, was there, and so was Roger Staubach, who had won the Heisman Trophy while playing for Navy before winning two Super Bowls as the quarterback of the Dallas Cowboys.

Tamara and Bobby went to get them drinks, and Stevie saw a table with food heaped high in the middle of the room.

"*That's* where I'm going," he said.

"How gallant of you to offer to get me food," Susan Carol said, her voice dripping with both her southern accent and sarcasm.

"I'll get you something," he said. "Find some space and I'll get the food and find you."

"I know you'll get the food," she said. "I'm just not convinced it will make it to me. But it's okay. I don't want to wait in line anyway."

She pointed to a life-size cutout of Roger Staubach that was part of the decoration for the party. "I'll be over there with Mr. Staubach. You won't be able to miss me."

"I *always* miss you," he said with a smile, and turned in the direction of the food.

Susan Carol watched him go. He was looking very handsome in the same jacket and tie he had worn to the White House.

As she walked toward the Staubach cutout, she ran into Tony Kornheiser, the former *Post* columnist turned TV host, and Phil Mickelson, the star golfer.

"Susan Carol," Kornheiser said. "Good to see you. Have you met Phil Mickelson?"

"No, I haven't," she said, shaking his hand. "It's certainly a pleasure."

"Tony says you're only fourteen and that you write better than anyone at the *Post* or the *Herald*," Mickelson said.

"Oh, that's not true at all," she said, blushing. "Why, Bobby Kelleher and Tamara Mearns and Sally Jenkins—"

"Are hacks," Kornheiser said. "Okay, not hacks. They're all my friends. I love them all. But they're all so unfair to Dan Snyder."

Mickelson turned to Kornheiser. "I hear you're about the only person in town who likes Dan Snyder."

Kornheiser paused. "Not true. His wife likes him . . . I think."

"Why don't *you* write anymore, Mr. Kornheiser?" Susan Carol asked.

"I'm a yodeler now, a minstrel, a circus act."

"Michael Wilbon still writes," Susan Carol said.

"Yeah, well, he's younger than me. And he can write a column in five minutes. I need more time than that."

They chatted for another moment before someone dragged Mickelson off. Apparently one of the local sports anchors was going to "die" if she didn't get to meet Mickelson. "Never seen Army-Navy before," he said as his PR person tugged on his arm. "I loved the stories in today's paper. Keep it up."

Susan Carol could see that Stevie had gotten to the point in the line where he had a plate in his hands and was waiting for people in front of him to put salad on their plates. She knew all he wanted to do was get to the guy carving the red meat.

She had spotted two more Heisman Trophy winners in the crowd—Navy's Joe Bellino and Army's Pete Dawkins—before Stevie made it back to her with some food. Just in time: the three Heisman winners were all introduced to the crowd, and honor was paid to Army's two other Heisman winners, Doc Blanchard and Glenn Davis, who had passed away.

When it was Staubach's turn to speak, he thanked everyone for being there and talked about how great it was that Army-Navy was being played in the nation's capital and how proud he was to be part of the Army-Navy rivalry.

"I can still vividly remember being introduced before my first Super Bowl as a starter thirty-eight years ago," he said. "As I ran out of the tunnel, I heard the public address announcer say, 'And at quarterback, from the United States Naval Academy, Roger Staubach!'" He paused. "Hearing him say 'from the United States Naval Academy' was the proudest moment of my life."

The entire crowd—Army people and Navy people—gave him a standing ovation when he finished.

Once the official program was done, everyone went back to mingling and the noise level shot through the roof. Stevie went off for seconds at the buffet, and Susan Carol was debating getting refills on their drinks when a short man in a dark suit walked up to her. She recognized the face, but she wasn't sure exactly why.

"Susan Carol Anderson," he said. "What a pleasure to meet you."

Susan Carol knew sarcasm when she heard it. He wasn't smiling, and he didn't offer his hand.

"I'm sorry," she said. "Do I know you?"

"You should know me, shouldn't you? After all, you've slandered me and my colleagues in the newspaper repeatedly the last two weeks."

Now she recognized the face. It was Mike Daniels, the referee from the Notre Dame game.

"First of all, Mr. Daniels, if I'd written something about y'all that was untrue, it would be libel, not slander," she said, trying to deal with this on a technical level and avoid the emotional.

"Look, kid, don't get smart with me. Do you have any idea of the trouble you've caused? Sure, it's easy to watch from the sidelines and review things in slo mo and second-guess the calls. But *you* try being out there with the play unfolding fast and getting every call right."

"I did point that out in my story—"

"Oh yeah, right before you called me and my crew

criminals." Daniels moved closer to her. He was no more than five foot seven, so Susan Carol was looking straight down at him. But she still felt herself shaking a little bit. "You called us all cheaters," he went on, poking his finger in her face, "and we don't have to put up with that. We don't get paid enough for this kind of harassment, and—"

Susan Carol was about to answer when she heard a voice behind her. "Is there a problem here?"

It was Stevie.

"Who the hell are you?" Daniels said.

"I'm the guy who is going to knock you across the room if you don't leave my girlfriend alone."

Daniels eyed Stevie, looking at his name tag. "You're the other kid reporter those idiots at the *Post* and *Herald* are letting write this week."

"That's right," he said, moving in front of Susan Carol, pushing Daniels backward in the process. "And if you don't back off right now, I'm going to write about how you spent the night before the big game getting drunk and threatening young girls."

"Why, you little—"

Daniels was cut off as two guys came up from behind him and tried to pull him away.

"C'mon, Mike, it's not worth it," one said.

"Calm down, or you'll blow everything," said the other.

Daniels shook off his friends' restraining arms, but he did step back.

"You two. You're the perfect . . . couple," he said.

Then he and his friends disappeared into the crowd.

"Well, he finally got a call right," Stevie said.

"What?"

He put his arm around her. "We *are* the perfect couple."

Susan Carol smiled at that, but she was still shaking. "I think I want to go home," she said.

"Let's find Bobby and Tamara," he said, nodding.

They found them talking to a girl who appeared to be about their age, Matt Rennie, and Bob Woodward.

"Stevie, Susan Carol, I'm glad you're here," Woodward said. "This is Sarah Strum. She won a writing contest at her high school and is spending a day shadowing me. But she would much rather meet the two of you."

"I'm a freshman like you two are," Sarah said. "But I still want to be like you when I grow up. You are *so* lucky."

Susan Carol wasn't feeling that lucky at the moment.

They made small talk for a while before Susan Carol said, "Bobby, I don't want to seem rude, but I don't feel well."

Kelleher seemed to understand that something was wrong. "Let's go get our coats," he said.

They said good night to Woodward and Sarah Strum and headed for the front door. It was definitely time to go home.

"So what happened back there?" Kelleher asked once they were all in the car. Susan Carol told him about Mike Daniels, his threatening tone, his mistaking libel for slander, and Stevie's bravery.

Kelleher looked at Mearns. "I don't like it. This guy's a loose cannon. Maybe the kids should report from the press box tomorrow."

"What?!!" Stevie and Susan Carol both said together. "No way!"

"I know, but . . . Tamara? What do you think?"

"I think they deserve the chance to finish their reporting as planned," she said. "And I also think we need to make sure they aren't left alone for a second."

Kelleher sighed. "Okay," he said. "Okay. This game has more drama than even I feel good about."

GAME DAY: 10 MINUTES
BEFORE KICKOFF

"**L**adies and gentlemen," the public address announcer boomed, "please welcome to the 111th playing of the Army-Navy game the president of the United States!" The cheers grew louder with every step he took. The only ones not cheering or clapping, Stevie noticed, were the Secret Service agents, whose heads appeared to be on swivels, and the photographers and TV cameramen backpedaling in front of President Obama as he smiled and waved and made his way to midfield.

"Okay," Pete Dowling said when the final notes of "Hail to the Chief" died away, "you guys be ready to move on my signal. Remember to stay close to me and, Stevie, no smart comments while they're doing the toss of the coin, okay?"

"Me?" Stevie said.

Dowling turned to another agent and pointed at Kelleher and Mearns. "They're fine right here during the toss," he said. "They stay here until the president leaves the field and Bob and I come back to get them."

The agent nodded. The noise hadn't abated even a little bit. "Hang on one minute," Dowling said to Stevie and Susan Carol. "Let the captains get out there first."

The captains had started walking to greet one another while their teammates, all wanting to get as close as they could, followed a few yards behind. Mike Daniels was waiting for them, and the president arrived a moment later. It was now extremely crowded around the giant Army-Navy logo at midfield.

Daniels introduced himself and the other six officials who would call the game. Agents were everywhere. Two CBS camera crews were moving around trying to get close-ups of everyone. Dowling pointed Stevie and Susan Carol to a spot a few feet from the Army captains. The president saw them and waved as if he had just spotted one of his kids at a school concert. They waved back.

"Don't move, don't say anything," Dowling said over the din. "Just watch and listen."

Stevie knew that as a reporter he should just be observing, but he was also an American and this was amazingly cool. He didn't even try to keep the grin off his face.

Daniels had now opened his microphone so everyone in the stadium could hear him.

"Mr. President, I'm Mike Daniels, the game referee. It's an honor to meet you, sir."

"It's great to be here," the president answered, standing close enough to the mike that he could be heard clearly.

"Mr. President, this is a special coin made for today's game," Daniels said, reaching into his pocket and removing an extremely large coin. "As you can see, the front of the coin has an image of the White House, the back of the coin shows the Capitol building. I'm going to give you the coin to toss."

"Thank you," President Obama said, taking the coin.

Daniels waved the four captains closer. The two Army captains stood with their backs to the Army sideline, their teammates bunched up behind them. The Navy captains faced them, and the president stood directly in between them.

Daniels said, "Gentlemen, I know you've all met the president. Navy is the visiting team this year. Mr. Dobbs, Mr. Middleton, which of you will call the toss?"

"I will," Dobbs said.

Stevie could see all the various cameramen, assembled opposite President Obama, jostling for position, clicking their cameras madly. He looked at Susan Carol for a split second and saw she had a smile as wide as his.

"Mr. President, will you hold the coin out so that Mr. Dobbs can see it?" Daniels asked.

President Obama held it in his palm and Daniels

continued. "Mr. Dobbs, the White House is heads." He looked at Obama, who turned the coin over in his hand. "And the Capitol building is tails," Daniels said. "Everyone understand?"

Everyone nodded. Daniels asked the captains to take a step back to give the president some room, and he took a step back himself to make sure the TV cameras had a clear shot of the president flipping the coin.

"Mr. President, whenever you are ready, you can flip the coin. Just toss it in the air and let it land on the ground."

The president smiled. "Good luck to all of you," he said, and flipped the coin high in the air.

Dobbs called, "Heads!" as the coin was spiraling in the air.

When the coin landed, Daniels looked down and said, "It's tails. Army wins the toss. Mr. Klein? What does your team want to do?"

"We'll defer," Derek Klein said, meaning Army would kick off to start the game so it could receive at the start of the second half.

Everyone moved around so Daniels could signal which direction Army would kick in. There was more hand-shaking all around. Everyone had been instructed to stay in place until the president left the field.

He was greeted by Lieutenant General Hagenbeck, the superintendent of West Point, and other Army officials and escorted to the Army side of the field, where he would watch the first half of the game. As ever, they were surrounded by camera crews and agents, but the president chatted happily with Hagenbeck, seeming completely at ease.

As soon as the president hit the sidelines, everyone on the field began scrambling again.

"Come on," Dowling said. "Let's get the field cleared so these guys can play a football game."

Oh yeah, Stevie thought, the game.

The plan was for Stevie and Susan Carol to watch the game from the sidelines: Stevie on the Army side, Susan Carol on the Navy side.

As the field was being cleared, Daniels paused as he passed them.

"You two better watch yourselves. If you get in the way *at all*, I can have you thrown out of here in about five seconds," he said.

"No, you can't," Pete Dowling said, magically appearing behind them. "I'm sure you have somewhere you need to be right now."

Daniels glared for an instant, then turned and jogged away.

"Thanks, Mr. Dowling," Susan Carol said.

"Can you two stay out of trouble for the next few hours, please?" Dowling said. "I don't want to have to protect you too."

"They're the ones who started it," Stevie said.

"I know," Dowling said. "Although actually, Susan Carol, your story started it. Not that it was wrong."

They heard another roar and saw that the president was giving a last wave before ducking into the tunnel. Dowling put his hand up to his ear again and said, "Roger that," into his wrist.

He nodded at Stevie and Susan Carol. "All clear. You guys get set up on the sidelines and *please* duck behind someone if one of the officials comes close to you."

"We will," Susan Carol said. "But what happened with the Arnott family?"

Dowling shrugged. "Nothing. They're in the stadium now, and we've got eyes on them. But there's nothing suspicious we can see. Seems that all their big talk was just that."

"But you had to take it seriously, right?" Stevie said.

Dowling nodded. "No doubt. Every threat is serious until proven otherwise. The FBI will continue to monitor their group. I appreciate your not writing anything that would compromise the agents' position."

"So you don't have any concerns about the rest of the game?" Susan Carol asked.

"Well, the president will change sides at halftime, and the job isn't done until we deliver him safely back to the White House. But no, I don't have any special concerns anymore."

"I do," said Stevie. "The refs still suck."

KICKOFF!

As Army kicker Jay Parker teed the ball up and the crowd came to its feet in anticipation of the kickoff, Susan Carol took a deep breath and looked around her at the happy, excited, tense, organized chaos of the Navy sideline. At last, they were going to see a football game. It had been a long two weeks and a very long morning. At least, she thought, the afternoon would be fun.

Alex Teich returned the kickoff for Navy to the 33-yard line. From there, Dobbs and his offense began moving the ball swiftly down the field. Fullback Alex Murray carried twice for twelve yards. Dobbs sprinted around the right side for nine and then went left for six and another first down. A quick slant pass to slotback G. G. Greene was good for another first down, and then Murray picked up another eight, setting up second and two at the Army 21. The Navy sideline was ebullient. They were poised to jump to a quick lead en route to a ninth straight win over Army.

Susan Carol could barely hear anything above the crowd and the constant strains of "Anchors Aweigh." Captain Matt Klunder joined them on the sidelines just as Dobbs took the snap and turned to hand the ball to Murray again. Only this time he pulled the ball out of Murray's stomach at the last possible second, took three quick steps back, and lofted the ball toward the end zone, where wide receiver Greg Jones was a good five yards behind all the Army defenders. Jones gathered the ball in and went into the end zone for a touchdown.

The Navy bench exploded.

But just as quickly, the cheer turned to a groan. Susan Carol saw Daniels consulting with the back judge and nodding.

"Holding, number 84," Daniels said, referring to Jones, the receiver who had caught the pass. "That's a ten-yard penalty, and we'll repeat second down."

Jeff Fair, Navy's trainer, was livid. "Holding? No Army player got close enough to the kid to get held."

"Oh, please," Klunder said. "Please don't let the refs steal another game—not *this* game."

"Let's not worry yet," Susan Carol said. "That's not one of the officials from the Notre Dame game."

"They really should have changed the officials," Fair said.

The penalty put Navy back to the Army 32. Dobbs

tried a screen pass on second down, but it went nowhere. On third down he tried to give the ball to Murray on a late draw, but the play only picked up a yard. Trying to get some momentum back, Kenny Niumatalolo decided to go for it on fourth down and eleven, but a pass to Greene in the end zone was broken up.

From the Army sidelines, Stevie watched as Army took over the ball and began its first drive of the game. The sophomore quarterback Trent Steelman was running the option offense nearly as smoothly as Dobbs. The Cadets picked up three quick first downs and were soon at the Navy 30. Steelman sprinted left with the ball and made a last-second pitch to slotback Steve Carpenter. Carpenter caught the ball with a full head of steam and raced to the Navy 5-yard line.

Dick Hall and Dean Taylor were high-fiving as the Army bench went crazy.

"Hang on, fellas," Tim Kelly said. "Take a look."

Sure enough, a yellow flag was lying on the turf not that far from where they were standing. This time the umpire had made the call. As Daniels opened his mike to indicate that left guard Joel Davis had been called for a hold, Taylor was screaming at him.

"How do you see a guard holding in the middle of the line on a pitch?" he asked. "What was that, a makeup call?"

Stevie made himself scarce behind Dick Hall as the ref

glared in their direction. The ball was being marched back to the Navy 40. Instead of a first and goal at the 5, it was first and twenty at the 40.

"You called it, Tim," Hall said. "The score is tied. One bad call each."

Stevie looked at the scoreboard. The first quarter was almost over and the score *was* tied: 0–0.

It stayed that way as the first quarter melted into the second. Both teams would make good yardage, but then the defenses seemed to really dig in when they were in the red zone and no one could score. At one point, Army's Derek Klein intercepted a Dobbs pass on a quick out pattern and raced thirty-nine yards down the field for a touchdown. But before the Army people could even begin celebrating, Stevie spotted the flag: interference on Klein. Army coach Rich Ellerson was beside himself: "There wasn't anything close to contact," he was screaming at the side judge who had made the call.

Navy took possession again, but nerves were high and the Mids got stalled by consecutive penalties for having a man in motion.

"Well, give them credit," Kelly said. "The refs are calling bad penalties equally on both teams."

The game was halted for a TV time-out. Stevie glanced at the scoreboard: there was 3:21 until halftime, and the game was still scoreless.

Terry Ramspeth, the line judge, had walked over near

where Stevie was standing during the time-out. He was, Stevie suspected, giving him the evil eye, but Stevie was doing his best to keep calm and look the other way. Dean Taylor, standing next to him, was a bit more of a hothead on the sidelines, as usual.

"What's your problem?" he yelled at Ramspeth. "Why don't you stop staring at the kid and focus on the game?"

"Settle down, Coach," Ramspeth said.

"I'm not a coach," Taylor said. "Am I wearing a headset?"

Ramspeth didn't have an answer for that one, and Taylor kept going. "How many more phantom calls are you guys going to make today?" he asked. "Are you going to make sure NO ONE scores in this game?"

Taylor had clearly hit a nerve. Ramspeth walked right up to him and said, "Okay, that's it," and threw a flag into the air. Daniels instantly trotted over.

"What've you got, Terry?" he asked.

"I don't even know who this guy is," he said. "But he's wearing Army gear and he's screaming profanities at me. Unsportsmanlike conduct."

"Profanities?" Taylor said. "That's an absolute lie."

Rich Ellerson came sprinting down the sideline. "What's going on with you guys, Mike? You're throwing flags on my team doc?"

"Terry says he used profanity."

Taylor cut in. "Complete and utter lie."

Hall and Kelly jumped in too. "No way," they both said. "He was talking to him, but there was no cursing."

Stevie wanted to back Taylor up too, but he figured he'd better keep his mouth shut.

"Give me a minute," said Daniels, who pulled Ramspeth away to talk. It looked like a heated conversation—Ramspeth was waving his arms; Daniels kept putting his palms downward to indicate he needed to calm down. Finally Daniels nodded and stepped clear of Ramspeth and opened his microphone.

Pulling *his* flag from his back pocket, he waved it in the air. "There is no flag," he said simply. Then he trotted over to Ellerson. "I'm cutting you some slack because it's an emotional game. But one more word from your sideline and the flag will stick."

Ellerson nodded but didn't say anything until the officials walked away. Then he turned to Taylor, Kelly, and Hall, his voice surprisingly soft. "You guys need to cool it. Doesn't matter how right you are and how wrong they are. We can't afford an unsportsmanlike in a scoreless game."

They all nodded as Daniels blew his whistle to put the ball back in play.

Taylor was still shaking his head five minutes later. "Man, usually refs are thicker-skinned than that. Guy went nuts, didn't he?"

Stevie smiled. "Well, you did imply he wasn't going to let anyone score."

Dicky Hall laughed. "Yeah, but he's said much worse and never gotten that strong a reaction."

"Much worse," Tim Kelly agreed.

"Hey!" Taylor protested. "Whose side are you on?"

Stevie laughed with them but then suddenly froze. What if . . . ?

"I'll be back in a minute," Stevie told his friends, and as Army came out of the huddle to resume play, he began running down the field to the end zone so he could cross to the Navy side. Susan Carol was standing with two men in Navy uniforms when he got there.

"Hey, you. Can you believe this game?" she said. "At least neither team can say the refs are cheating them. Every time one team gets a bad call, then the other one does too."

Stevie was a bit winded, so he didn't respond right away. "Tell me again what your dad told you about betting and the over-under?"

Susan Carol shot him a look as Steelman picked up four yards and the crowd on the sideline moved away from them to follow the play.

"What—?"

"Just repeat it for me."

She sighed but did as asked. "If you bet the over-under, the bookie picks a number and you say whether the total score for both teams will be more or less than that number. What is this about?"

"What's the score?" Stevie asked.

"Nothing-nothing."

"And what's happened every time someone gets close to scoring?"

She opened her mouth to answer and then stopped. "Oh my God!" she said. "Every time someone has had a chance to score, there's been a penalty."

Steelman threw an incomplete pass in the direction of Michael Arnott, leaving Army at third and six.

"It's the perfect solution, right?" Stevie said. "Everyone sits back and says, 'Well, the officiating may be bad, but it's been bad both ways.' They can't use the same tack as at Notre Dame. This way they can control the game without making anyone suspicious."

"Do you *really* think . . . ?"

"*Yes*," Stevie said. "I do."

Army was lining up to punt, having failed to pick up a first down. There was 2:14 left in the half, and Navy had called time out hoping to get good field position and put together some kind of drive in those last two minutes. TV had taken yet another time-out for more commercials.

"What do we do?" Susan Carol asked. "How could we prove it? We can't just walk into the referees' locker room at halftime and accuse them of bettin' on the game."

"No, we can't. But the Secret Service and the FBI can. You know there are FBI agents here today. There have to be. And fixing a game is a federal offense."

She pulled out her cell phone and began dialing.

"Who're you calling?"

"Mr. Dowling." She paused. "Mr. Dowling, I know this sounds crazy, but are there FBI people here today?" She paused again. "Is there any way you can meet us in the tunnel near the referees' locker room? Like now?"

Dowling said something in response and Susan Carol nodded. "I swear I wouldn't bother you if it was.

"Okay, thank you. We'll walk over there right now."

She snapped the phone shut. "He can't come himself because the president is going to cross the field soon. But he's sending two FBI guys to meet us."

"Wow," Stevie said. "I guess he trusts us a little, anyway."

She nodded. "I know—I hope we're right about this." Stevie smiled, and then she said, "Wait, I mean, I wish we were wrong, of course, but I hope we're right. . . ."

"I know what you mean," he said. "Let's go."

They jogged in the direction of the tunnel, stopping in the end zone to watch Army punt. Navy came with a ten-man rush, trying to block the punt. Someone broke through the middle and ran right at punter Kyle Delahooke. Stevie saw the ball come off Delahooke's foot and smack into the Navy defender's outstretched hands. The ball careened off his hands to the right and there was a mad scramble for it.

A Navy player scooped it up—Stevie saw it was number 15—and ran toward the end zone. As he crossed the goal line, the Navy sideline exploded.

But Susan Carol was shaking her head. "Look," she said, pointing across the field.

Sure enough, there was a flag.

"Would you like to bet this call goes against Navy?"

"Oh no," Stevie said. "I'm not a betting man."

Mike Daniels was consulting with line judge Terry Ramspeth and solemnly nodded.

"Offside," he said. "On the defense. It's a five-yard penalty. Repeat fourth down."

Stevie looked down the sideline just in time to see Kenny Niumatalolo steaming toward Daniels, headset off, screaming. "Who was it?" he demanded. "What number? You didn't even give a number! What game are you guys watching out there?"

"Come on," Susan Carol said. "Let's go find the FBI."

They took off for the tunnel, where guards and Secret Service agents were posted, blocking people from coming onto the field.

"If you leave now, you can't come back until the president has crossed the field," someone in a suit warned them.

"It's okay," Stevie said. "We understand."

They turned the corner and ran for the officials' locker room.

Two men in dark suits were waiting.

"Are you Steve and Susan Carol?" one of them said. He was very tall, with short-cropped dark hair.

"That's us," Susan Carol said.

"I'm Agent Mayer; this is Agent Caccese," the tall one said. "What have you kids got?"

"Your theory, Stevie," Susan Carol said. "Tell them."

Stevie did, talking as fast as he could about all the calls

and about Ramspeth's reaction when Dean Taylor had mentioned making sure no one scored.

Mayer looked at Caccese. "What do you think?"

"I've heard crazier theories that have been proven out," Caccese said. "And after all the fuss at the Notre Dame game, we've been watching for anomalies here. Gamblers come in all shapes and sizes."

"And stripes," Mayer added.

Caccese rolled his eyes and pulled out his cell.

"Tom, when the officials come off, stall them a minute. Tell them the service is sweeping their locker room one more time."

"What're you going to do?" Stevie asked.

"I'm going to put a bug in their locker room," Caccese said. "See if they say anything interesting during halftime. I'll need about fifteen minutes to get it done."

After a few more phone calls and about five minutes, four more FBI guys appeared, two carrying suitcases. Also two Secret Service agents and two bomb-sniffing dogs. The six of them walked to the door of the officials' locker room and knocked while Mayer, Caccese, Stevie, and Susan Carol held back in the hallway. Todd, the attendant, answered. Stevie couldn't hear what the FBI and Secret Service agents said, but he heard Todd say, "There are only twenty-two seconds left in the half; the guys'll be in here in about two minutes."

Whatever was said in response, Todd came out and the six men and two dogs went in. Todd leaned against the wall and shook his head.

The half ended while they were waiting. Stevie and Susan Carol shrank back behind Mayer and Caccese while the seven officials walked past, escorted by several yellow-jacketed security men, but none of them looked left or right as they walked.

When they got to the door and saw Todd, Mike Daniels said, "What're you doing out here?"

Todd pointed at the door. "Secret Service is in there. They said they had to have the dogs check one more time."

"Why?" Daniels asked. "The president isn't coming anywhere near here again."

"Ask them," Todd said.

At that point, Agent Caccese walked down the hallway to Daniels.

"I'm sorry, sir, it's strictly procedure when the president is still in the building. We rechecked the team locker rooms and everything else on this level too. It shouldn't be more than another minute."

"We need to get in there and prepare for the second half," Daniels said.

"I understand. If you need, we can delay the start of the second half for an extra couple minutes."

The door opened at that moment and the Secret Service men with the dogs came out first. The FBI guys—who Stevie hoped looked no different from the Secret Service guys to the refs—followed.

"All clear," an agent said to Caccese. Turning to

Daniels, he said, "Sorry for the delay. We won't need to bother you again."

The officials made their way into the locker room and Todd followed. If any of the officials had spotted Stevie and Susan Carol, they gave no indication of it.

Caccese walked back to them and Agent Mayer.

"It's all set. We've got people in the command center listening, and we'll go back there now. We'll let you know if we hear anything."

"Thank you," they said, just as strains of "Hail to the Chief" began again.

"Any way you can help us get back on the field to watch this?" Susan Carol asked. "We'd really like to see it."

Caccese nodded. "Tom, take them out and see what you can do, will you? I'll meet you back in the command center in five minutes."

"Follow me, guys," Mayer said.

He led them to the tunnel, which was blocked. "I've got two who have clearance from Pete Dowling to go back out," he said.

Apparently those were the magic words. Mayer walked them onto the field. "You'll be okay from here," he said. "We'll talk soon."

Stevie checked the scoreboard clock and saw there were still twenty minutes left in the break.

He could see that the president had just reached the field. Representatives from the army, the navy, and the marines lined both sides of the 50-yard line; all of them snapped to attention. As the president passed each person, he or she saluted.

Stevie could see Army superintendent Hagenbeck walking with the president, who was trailed by several other people in uniform, a number of Secret Service agents, and the usual phalanx of photographers and TV camera crews. Right at midfield were the representatives from Navy.

"I'm glad we got to see this," Stevie said to Susan Carol.

"Me too," she said. "But I wonder what's going on in that referees' locker room."

Stevie wondered too. The president had reached midfield. The army officers snapped off salutes that were returned by their Navy counterparts. The president shook hands with the Army people and then joined the Navy people, who turned around to escort him to their sidelines. The entire stadium had come to its feet on both sides, applauding the scene.

"What do we do now?" Stevie asked as the president reached the other side of the field.

"We watch the halftime show," Susan Carol said. "And we wait."

IT'S OFFICIAL

The two bands put on an impressive halftime show, each ending its performance with the school fight song, which brought everyone back to their feet. Normally, Stevie would have enjoyed every minute of it, but he was squirming, looking at the clock every ten seconds, finding it hard to believe time could move so slowly.

The Army band cleared the field and the players came back out. And much to Stevie's disappointment—so did the officials. Stevie and Susan Carol were both standing on the Army sideline. The clock was under two minutes. Apparently the second half would start on time.

"What do you think?" he asked Susan Carol.

"No idea," she said.

Just as she finished, Stevie saw Pete Dowling, Bob Campbell, and the two FBI agents, Mayer and Caccese, coming out of the tunnel. Dowling spotted them, pointed at them, and the four men began walking briskly in their direction.

"Think we're in trouble?" Stevie asked.

"We'll find out soon," Susan Carol said, sounding a little bit shakier than Stevie would have hoped.

Dowling spoke first when the four men reached them.

"Your theory might be right," he said. "But we can't be sure."

"What do you mean?" Susan Carol asked.

Dowling looked at Caccese, who filled them in. "We definitely heard some things that sound suspicious. The referee—is it Daniels?—was lecturing someone about keeping his cool, that getting into arguments with people on the sidelines didn't help anything."

"That would have been Ramspeth," Stevie said.

"Right," Caccese said. "There was also talk about just sticking with what they were doing and being close to the payoff."

"Payoff?" Susan Carol said. "You've got it right there, don't you?"

Caccese shook his head. "No. They *might* be talking about some kind of bet; they could also just be talking about getting paid for working the game or the payoff of knowing they've done a good job. Trust me, it would never hold up in court. Bugging the room without a court order is already a little shaky. But we called Ed Murphy, who heads up our gambling unit in DC, and he thought there was cause. He's on his way now."

Caccese finished, "My gut tells me you guys have this

right. We just don't have enough evidence to take any action."

Stevie felt his heart sink.

"The room is still bugged," Mayer said. "Maybe we'll hear something when they come in afterward. And we'll watch to see if any of these guys seems to come into windfalls after the game. It's not over."

"But the game is," Susan Carol said.

"Yeah," Mayer said. "Could be. I'm truly sorry."

Stevie and Susan Carol decided to stick together on the sidelines, if only to take solace in each other's company. They started on the Army sideline since Army had the football to start the second half.

The third quarter was like a rerun of the first two. Army moved the ball quickly into Navy territory and had a third and one at the Navy 37. Fullback Jared Hassin, Stevie's old friend who had piled into him at West Point, dove into the line and appeared to pick up the first down. In came Ramspeth—the line judge—to spot the ball. He picked it up and moved it back almost a full yard from where Hassin had been tackled. The Army bench immediately began screaming about the spot.

"What is with these guys?" Dean Taylor said. "It's that same guy again, the line judge."

Ramspeth's spot left Army a yard short of a first down.

"I'm going to tell you something right now," Stevie said while Ellerson called a time-out to decide whether to go for it on fourth and one or punt. "If you go for it and get the first down, there will be a penalty."

Taylor, Hall, and Kelly all looked at him. "You just being cynical, Steve?" Hall asked.

"I don't think he is," Kelly said before Stevie could answer.

Army decided to go for the first down. They lined up in a tight formation, apparently planning to either quarterback sneak or go for the fullback dive again. Just as Steelman took the snap, though, the whistle blew. In came Daniels.

"Illegal motion before the snap," he said. "That's a five-yard penalty. Repeat fourth down."

As the umpire picked the ball up and moved it back five yards, it was Ellerson's turn to demand to know who the penalty was on. Daniels pretended not to hear.

"They didn't even wait to see if we made it," Taylor said.

"Guess they didn't want to take any chances," Susan Carol said.

With the play now fourth and six, Army punted, the ball rolling out-of-bounds on the 4-yard line.

"That should make the officials happy," Susan Carol said. "They've killed five minutes, and Navy's ninety-six yards from the goal line."

"What do you guys know?" Tim Kelly said. "You know something."

"We might," Stevie said. "We just aren't sure."

"More sure by the minute, though," Susan Carol added.

TV had gone to time-out. As the cadets and the midshipmen in the stands whooped it up, Stevie saw Mayer, Caccese, Dowling, and Campbell running down the sidelines.

"We've got them," Caccese said as they got close.

"Whaaaa?" they both said.

"No time for details right now," Caccese said. "But you know the kid in the locker room, the one taking care of the officials?"

"Daniels's nephew, Todd?" Stevie said.

"Yeah. As soon as the boys left the locker room for the second half, he was on the phone with offshore betting services. He was reading off confirmation numbers to make sure the bets they'd placed before the game were all in place. Based on what we've heard, these guys have at least ten million dollars riding on the under—which was forty-eight points—and even more riding on the regulation game ending scoreless."

"So what are you going to do?" Stevie asked.

"Ed Murphy, the head of the gambling unit, just arrived," Caccese said. "We asked the TV producer to hold the time-out for a minute longer so we can remove these guys."

"Remove them?" Stevie and Susan Carol shouted together.

"Yup. They can leave the field voluntarily or in

handcuffs. We're drawing up warrants for their arrests right now in the command center."

"But are you sure all seven are involved?" Stevie asked.

"Not a hundred percent. Todd used eight different names when confirming the bets. They were fake names, but we're pretty sure it's these seven guys plus him. Okay, here comes Murph."

A tall man with iron-gray hair in an equally gray suit was walking toward them, followed by at least a dozen other agents.

"Which one is the referee, John?" he asked, all business.

Caccese pointed at Daniels, who was in conversation at that moment with the umpire. "I'll ask the Army coach to call him over."

"Let's go," Murphy said.

Murphy, Caccese, and Mayer began walking up the Army sideline with a squad of agents trailing behind them. From the stands it must have looked very strange, Stevie thought. The FBI approached Ellerson, who took off his headset. There was a brief nod and then he waved at Daniels, who trotted over.

Stevie was dying to hear the conversation, but Daniels's body language was clear enough. As Murphy began speaking, he lurched backward. Then he was shouting.

If any of it bothered Murphy, it didn't show, and he cut him off effectively. With the crowd beginning to murmur, Daniels waved the other officials over. Stevie saw

Ken Niumatalolo several yards onto the field on his side, clearly confused by what the commotion could be. After a few more seconds of discussion, which included Terry Ramspeth screaming while taking his cap off and throwing it onto the ground, the FBI men and the officials began walking off the field.

The fans didn't know how to react. Some booed. Others hooted. Mostly there was confused silence. Murphy pointed at Pete Dowling, who nodded and began talking into his wrist. Within a minute Stevie knew what he had been saying.

"Ladies and gentlemen," the PA announcer said, "we apologize, but there will be a brief delay because there is a problem with the game officials."

"Yeah, there's a problem," Stevie heard a fan yell from the stands. "They SUCK!"

Dowling turned to Bob Campbell. "Bob, go tell Niumatalolo what's going on and that we're going to need a few minutes. They can keep their kids out here or take them back to the locker rooms. Whatever they want. Then meet me back in the tunnel; we've got the ADs en route."

Campbell nodded and took off across the field.

"You two can come too if you want," Dowling said. "You started all this. You have any brilliant ideas where we can find some new officials?"

* * *

Chet Gladchuk, the Navy athletic director, and Kevin Anderson, his counterpart at Army, were clearly confused when they arrived in the tunnel a few minutes later.

"What's going on?" Gladchuk asked. "The officials just went by me with a bunch of agents. Are they being arrested for incompetence or something?"

"Gentlemen, I'm sorry, but we've got a situation here," Agent Caccese said. "If those seven men had continued officiating, I can tell you with certainty that the game was going to end regulation at zero-zero."

"You aren't the first one to make that comment today," Anderson said. "What'd they do, bet the under?"

"That's about the size of it. We can get you details later," Caccese said. "For the moment, we need seven new officials for the game to continue. Any ideas?"

Gladchuk and Anderson both gaped at him.

"You're serious, aren't you?" Gladchuk said.

"As serious as someone trying to fix the Army-Navy game," Caccese answered.

"We could call Harold Neve at the ACC," suggested Anderson. But no one seemed to think he'd be all that helpful.

Stevie ventured, "Would the officials for the Redskins game tomorrow be in town already?"

"Maybe—but it would take a while to find out and get them here. And the NFL rules are different. . . ."

Everyone was quiet for a moment. Then Susan Carol said, "What about the high school officials? The ones honored before the game?"

Anderson snapped his fingers. "Of course. They're all up in a corporate box, watching the game."

"We need seven of them," Caccese said.

"What about uniforms?" Susan Carol asked.

"They have to keep spares in the locker room," Gladchuk said. "I'm sure someone who works here for the Redskins can help us with that."

Caccese looked at Anderson and Gladchuk. "No matter how good or bad they may be, at least they won't be cheating," he said.

Both athletic directors nodded. Then everyone pulled out their cell phones and started to dial.

It took about thirty minutes to sort out which of the high school officials would take over the game and to get them outfitted and ready. Agent Mayer returned to say that the seven officials and Todd were being taken to the FBI office downtown to be charged with game-fixing and assorted other gambling-related crimes. He and Dowling then went with the two athletic directors to explain the plan to the coaches.

The teams had both gone to the locker rooms, and the crowd was told nothing more than that the delay simply had to do with a problem with the officials. They would learn the rest soon enough, Stevie imagined. There were some murmurs, but no one was leaving, that was for sure. The weather was cold but not frigid, and the sun was shining down.

"That's one of the good things about a military crowd: they don't question things as much as some other people might," Kelleher said. He and Tamara had managed to get downstairs with their all-access passes after Stevie and Susan Carol had called to fill them in.

"I've never seen anything like it," Tamara said. "Stevie, what tipped you off? We were all sitting in the press box thinking it was a horribly reffed game but that at least the calls were balancing out."

"That's what I thought too," Stevie said. "But when the line judge went off on Dr. Taylor after he said something about keeping anyone from scoring, it seemed like an over-the-top reaction. Just like the way the officials over-reacted about Susan Carol's articles. Plus, I believed Susan Carol. She didn't see how those calls at the Notre Dame game could be honest mistakes, so I started to believe they were *dishonest* mistakes."

"And the kid Todd was stupid enough to make the call to confirm the bets from the locker room," Kelleher said. "That's unreal. He walks out into the hall and uses his cell phone, they never get caught."

"True," Susan Carol said. "But now they've got all those confirmation numbers on tape."

"Well, we've got to go upstairs and let our papers know what happened," Kelleher said. "I'm told the FBI is putting out a press release on the whole thing within an hour, but we can at least get some people moving downtown—checking out who these guys are, their backgrounds, things like that. You guys stay on the sidelines and focus on the game. We'll talk about how you'll write it when it's over. You may have to do something in the first person. Either way, you'll both have a lot to do."

They both nodded just as the new officials walked past, heading onto the field.

The teams were back out and had been given an extra couple of minutes to warm up after the long break.

Susan Carol had made her way back to the Navy sideline and found Captain Klunder waiting to shake her hand. "I hear we have you to thank for this, Susan Carol."

"No—it was Stevie who put it together, really," she tried to say, but then Ken Niumatalolo came up and lifted her off the ground in a bear hug.

"Looks like you were right," he said.

"More than I thought, even," Susan Carol said.

"Well, thank you for your story—and for sticking with it. You made all the difference. You saved the game—I can't even tell you—" One of his coaches called him away, and he ran back to get ready for the game to resume.

Before she could start to take that in, she felt a tap on her shoulder. She turned, and Ricky Dobbs bent down and kissed her on the cheek. "Thank you," he said. "For giving us back the game."

Then he put on his helmet and ran onto the field.

Suddenly, Susan Carol wished she had a place to sit down.

STARTING OVER

The rest of the second half was everything you could have wanted an Army-Navy game to be. If the officials made a mistake, neither side seemed to notice—these refs were every player's new best friend.

Navy, which had been backed up on its 4-yard line before the break, couldn't move and had to punt to Army, which took over at midfield. From there, the Cadets put together the first (allowed) scoring drive of the day, with quarterback Trent Steelman diving in from the 1-yard line. Navy answered right away, Dobbs matching his counterpart with his own run into the end zone, tying the game at 7–7 with 2:07 left in the third quarter.

It was Army's ball again, but Alan Arnott stepped in front of his brother, made a one-handed interception of a Steelman pass, and got the ball back for Navy on the Army 32. On the very first play, Dobbs faked to Murray, pulled the ball back at the last minute, and found Greg Jones wide open in the middle. It was the exact play that had produced the called-back touchdown in the first half. But this time there was no flag, and Navy led 14–7.

Undaunted, Steelman fired a blistering pass through two defenders to Michael Arnott, who outraced his brother and two other defenders while sprinting forty-seven yards to tie the game again as the third quarter ended.

"This is the way Army-Navy is supposed to be," Taylor said to Stevie. "You have your heart in your throat on every play."

After the gun sounded to end the third quarter—the new officials had apparently taken possession of Dowling's starter pistol—Stevie looked up and saw Susan Carol walking in his direction.

"What's up?" he asked.

"Nothing," she said. "I missed you. This is too good to watch without my partner."

The fourth quarter was the same as the third: back and forth. Navy put together a seven-minute drive to go up 21–14. Army responded by taking almost five minutes off the clock and tying the score again with 3:08 left.

Everyone in the stadium was on their feet. Dobbs, cool as ever, drove his team to the Army 33, finding slotback G. G. Greene on a key third and eight for twenty-seven yards. Two running plays moved the ball to the 24 with the clock ticking toward a minute. Army called time out with 1:21 to go.

"They don't want to let the clock run all the way down and let Navy kick a field goal to win the game at the buzzer," Susan Carol said.

"Then they have to stop them on this play, or that will happen," Stevie said.

For once, Kelly, Hall, and Taylor were all quiet. They knew what was at stake as Navy lined up on third and one. Dobbs brought his team up, waving for quiet from the Navy side. Navy didn't try anything fancy. Dobbs handed the ball to Murray to drive up the middle. But Army had seen it coming and Murray never got to the line of scrimmage. He struggled forward for a second but was brought down at the 25-yard line.

Army immediately used its second time-out. Navy had fourth and two with the clock showing 1:09.

"Any chance they go for it?" Stevie asked.

Susan Carol shook her head. "No. Navy's got a very good field goal kicker and Army's only goin' to have one time-out left either way. They go for the field goal here for sure."

As usual, she was right. Navy kicker Joe Buckley trotted out with the field goal unit.

"Maybe we should call time here to ice him," Hall said.

"Can't," Taylor said. "We need that last time-out when we get the ball back."

Buckley lined up for the kick. The snap was perfect and he calmly kicked the ball cleanly through the uprights. Navy led 24–21 with 1:05 left in the game.

Stevie could see the Navy sideline celebrating. He could also see Niumatalolo waving at his players to calm down. He knew the game wasn't over yet.

Stevie could feel a chill in the air. Because of the delay, it was now almost four o'clock and the field was bathed in shadows.

But no one in the stands cared a bit. They were on their feet, yelling full throttle.

"Who do you want to see win?" he yelled at Susan Carol over the noise.

"I don't know," Susan Carol yelled back. "I can't stand the thought of seeing either team lose."

Stevie felt the same way. He'd found it much harder to be a die-hard fan since he started covering sports. He always rooted for his friends to do well. But in this case, he had friends on both sidelines.

Navy kicked off, and Army kick returner John Conroy found a little hole on the right side and got the ball to the 36-yard line.

"Gives us a chance," Kelly said.

He was right.

Steelman ran an option to the right and picked up eleven yards and a first down. That stopped the clock with fifty-one seconds to go. On the next play, Army spiked the ball to stop the clock immediately.

"How far do you need to get the ball for Parker to have a chance at a field goal?" Stevie asked.

"Jay's made one from 50 this season," Hall said. "That's the longest of his career. We have to get to the 33."

Steelman ran left on the next play and pitched to Steve Carpenter. He picked up six, so they were in Navy territory now. On the 47. The clock was running and, because of the spike on first down, it was now third and four.

"Have to save the time-out as long as we can," Kelly said.

Steelman got a quick snap with twenty-nine seconds to go and, surprisingly, handed it to the fullback Hassin, who went straight up the middle. Navy was surprised too. Hassin had a huge hole and he picked up nine yards—and, most importantly, the first down—steamrolling to the 38. Again the clock stopped for the chains to be moved. Again Steelman spiked the ball on the next play. There were seventeen seconds left in the game.

Stevie looked back and saw Jay Parker calmly kicking the ball into a net a few yards from where he was standing.

Steelman took the snap again, faked to Hassin, and went back to try a play-action pass. Navy had gambled, though, and Middleton was coming fast on a safety blitz. Steelman never had a chance to get off a throw. Navy defenders took him down at the 46. The clock ticked under ten seconds.

Coach Ellerson took Army's last time-out with nine seconds left. It was third and eighteen. Army had to some-how pick up about twelve or thirteen yards to get into Parker's range *and* stop the clock so there'd be time to get the field goal team onto the field.

"I think they may be done," Susan Carol said.

"NEVER say that," said Taylor, who had overheard her.

Army came back to the line after the time-out. TV hadn't gone to commercial, so the time-out only lasted forty-five seconds. Steelman took the snap and quickly rolled to his right. He made a pump fake as if to throw deep, then threw a short sideline pass to Michael Arnott, who had curled underneath the Navy defense. Arnott caught the ball and was shoved out of bounds by his brother at the Navy 36. Stevie looked at the clock: there was one second left.

They had no choice but to hope that Parker could make the longest field goal of his life. He trotted onto the field.

"Well, at least we've got a shot at it," Hall said.

"It'll take a miracle," Kelly answered.

"Miracles happen," Taylor said.

As soon as Parker got into position to kick, Navy called time out. They had that luxury. In fact, they could call one more. Which they did. Parker had to wait close to two minutes before he finally had a chance to line up to kick. He was standing right on the 43-yard line, meaning he was fifty-three yards from the goalposts.

Susan Carol slipped her hand into Stevie's and he squeezed.

The snap came back and the ball went down. When it came off Parker's foot, Stevie thought it was wide right. But as it got closer to the goalposts, it was hooking. It hooked and hooked and began to wobble, and finally it hit the right goalpost—and bounced through!

It was good. Hall, Kelly, and Taylor were all pummeling each other. Susan Carol had her arm in the air and Stevie's along with it. The Army bench went wild, and the stadium was exploding on both sides.

They had played sixty minutes—almost twenty-five of them with real referees—and the score was tied 24–24.

They would decide the game in overtime.

"NOW WHAT?" Stevie said.

"Now we watch them go at it some more," she said. "Then we watch them stand together and cry during the alma maters no matter who wins the game."

"I don't want it to ever end," Stevie said.

She nodded, her eyes shining. "It's exactly the way it should be, isn't it?" She smiled. "And best of all, you and I get to watch it together."

As usual, she was right. Being a part of Army-Navy was like nothing else he'd ever done in his life. But seeing it up close with his arm around Susan Carol made it just about perfect.

A Historic Rivalry

The Army-Navy rivalry began in 1890 when Cadet Dennis Michie accepted a challenge from the Naval Academy and the two teams faced off on the Plain at West Point. Navy won that game 24–0 in front of a crowd of five hundred.

By 1893, the crowds had swelled to eight thousand, and stores and offices were closed in Annapolis so that people could attend the game.

But football then was a brutal game with few rules and many injuries. And the fans were just as violent! After Navy's victory in 1893, a rear admiral and a brigadier general got into a dispute about the game that nearly led to a duel. President Grover Cleveland stepped in and put a halt to the rivalry to try to defuse the situation.

But in 1897, Theodore Roosevelt, then assistant secretary of the navy, wrote an impassioned plea to have the game reinstated.

The rivalry picked up again in 1899 on neutral ground—at Franklin Field, in Philadelphia, where Army beat Navy 17–5 in front of a crowd of twenty-seven thousand.

In 1901, Theodore Roosevelt was president of the

United States, and he became the first president to attend the Army-Navy game—and he began the tradition of switching sides of the field at halftime.

Football was still a brutal sport, and there was talk of banning intercollegiate football altogether—especially after the 1905 season, in which there were nineteen fatalities nationwide. But President Roosevelt worked to enact new safety rules and require equipment to reduce casualties, keeping the game alive.

Here's How the Rivalry Stands After the 2009 Game

The Army-Navy game has been played 110 times.

Navy leads the series with 54 wins. Army has 49 wins. And 7 games have ended in a tie.

The biggest margin of victory came in 1973 when Navy shut out Army 51–0.

Navy is dominating the series right now—it has won the past eight games.

National Championships

The Cadets of Army and the Midshipmen of Navy have not contended for the national title in recent years. Both schools' exacting academic requirements and the players' military commitment following graduation mean that the teams are not made up of many NFL hopefuls. But both teams have had their powerhouse moments.

Army was national champion in 1914, 1944, and 1945—ending each of those years undefeated.

Navy holds a share of the 1926 national championship title—one of three undefeated teams that year.

Each of these championship teams was a standout.

In 1914, Army's victory over Navy capped its first un-defeated season. On the team that year as a student assistant was future president Dwight D. Eisenhower. Eisenhower was a running back and linebacker in 1912, but a knee injury following a tackle forced him off the field and onto the sidelines.

In 1926, the game was played in Chicago for the first—and only—time. Soldier Field was being dedicated as a monument to the servicemen who fought in World War I, and there seemed no more fitting way to mark this than with the Army-Navy game. Navy came into the game undefeated and Army had lost just once that year, to Notre Dame. The teams battled to a 21–21 tie before a crowd of over a hundred thousand.

The 1944 game was played during wartime, and the Army team traveled to Municipal Stadium in Baltimore by steamer ship—under escort from Navy warships guarding against submarine attacks. Army went into this game ranked number one in the country, and Navy was ranked number two. Army's 23–7 win gave them the national title. In order to get a ticket to this game, fans also had to purchase a war bond, and $58,637,000 was raised.

Both teams were ranked one and two the next year as well, and the 1945 game was labeled the "game of the century" before it was even played. Army won again—cementing their third national title. Playing in that game were two of Army's Heisman Trophy winners: Doc Blanchard and Glenn Davis.

Heisman Trophy Winners and Other Famous Players

Five players from Army and Navy have won the Heisman Trophy for the most outstanding collegiate football player of the year:

Doc Blanchard, Army, Fullback, 1945
Glenn Davis, Army, Halfback, 1946
Pete Dawkins, Army, Halfback, 1958
Joe Bellino, Navy, Halfback, 1960
Roger Staubach, Navy, Quarterback, 1963

Army boasts 24 players and 4 coaches in the College Football Hall of Fame.

Navy has 19 players and 3 coaches in the College Football Hall of Fame.

But only one player from either academy has gone on to the Pro Football Hall of Fame: Roger Staubach of Navy.

Thomas J. Hamilton, Navy class of 1927. Hamilton was a halfback on the 1926 national championship team. After serving on the USS *Enterprise* in World War II, he went on to be head coach and athletic director at both the Naval Academy and the University of Pittsburgh.

Doc Blanchard, Army class of 1947. During his three years playing for Army, his team's record was 27–0–1, with the one tie a famous 0–0 duel with Notre Dame. Notre Dame coach Ed McKeever was so impressed with Blanchard after Army's 59–0 win in 1944 that he said, "I've just seen Superman in the flesh. He wears number 35 and goes by the name of Blanchard." Blanchard and his teammate Glenn Davis were a devastating pair of rushers, with

Blanchard known as "Mr. Inside" to Davis's "Mr. Outside." They appeared together on the cover of *Time* magazine in 1945. That year, Blanchard won the Heisman Trophy, the Maxwell Award, and the James E. Sullivan Award. He was the first junior ever to win the Heisman. Blanchard was third overall in the 1946 NFL draft, but chose a military career instead. He became a fighter pilot with the air force and served in the Vietnam War. He retired from service in 1971 as a colonel.

Glenn Davis, Army class of 1947. This halfback was known as "Mr. Outside" and won the Maxwell Award in 1944 and the Heisman in 1946. In 1944, Davis led the nation with 120 points scored and 59 touchdowns. He averaged 8.3 yards per carry throughout his career, and during the 1945 season he averaged an amazing 11.5 yards per carry—both are records that still stand today. After serving in the military, Davis played for the Los Angeles Rams, but a knee injury ended his football career.

Pete Dawkins, West Point class of 1959. Dawkins won the Heisman Trophy and the Maxwell Award in 1958. He is the only cadet in history to simultaneously be a brigade commander, president of his class, captain of the football team, and a "star man"—in the top five percent of his class academically. Dawkins went on to be a Rhodes scholar, earning a degree from Oxford, and later earned a PhD from Princeton. Pete Dawkins served as a paratrooper and received two bronze stars during the Vietnam War. He ended his twenty-four-year military career as a brigadier general.

Joe Bellino, Navy class of 1961. Bellino won the Heisman Trophy in 1960. After serving in the military, he went on to play three seasons as a kick returner for the Boston Patriots. He has the somewhat dubious distinction of being the lowest-drafted Heisman winner in the history of the NFL.

Roger Staubach, Navy class of 1965. Staubach was hailed by Coach Wayne Hardin as "the best quarterback Navy ever had." He won both the Heisman Trophy and the Maxwell Award in 1963, and led his team to victory in two Army-Navy games. After completing his military commitment and serving in the Vietnam War, Staubach joined the Dallas Cowboys as a twenty-seven-year-old rookie, and went on to a Hall of Fame career. He played in four Super Bowls, won two, and was MVP of Super Bowl VI. That made him the first of only four players to win both the Heisman Trophy and a Super Bowl MVP.

Phil McConkey, Navy class of 1979. After serving his military commitment, McConkey signed with the New York Giants as a twenty-seven-year-old rookie. He was a wide receiver and kickoff and punt returner, and he played a key role in the Giants' Super Bowl XXI win in January 1987.

Napoleon McCallum, Navy class of 1985. McCallum was a star tailback and kick returner. He played for the Los Angeles Raiders while also serving in the Navy in 1986. He then left to complete his military service. He rejoined the team in 1990 and played until 1994, when a knee injury ended his football career.

Games Not Played

After the first Army-Navy matchup in 1890, there have been only ten years when the game was not played.

The game was suspended for five years from 1894 to 1898 by President Cleveland due to excessive violence and injury.

In 1909, Army canceled their football season after Cadet Eugene Byrne was killed during the Army-Harvard game.

The games in 1917 and 1918 were suspended for World War I.

The 1928 and 1929 games were canceled because of a dispute over player eligibility.

Where and When

The Army-Navy game was traditionally played on the Saturday after Thanksgiving, but the date has been pushed back so that it will be both the last game on Army's and

Navy's schedule and the last game of the regular college football season. It is now played on the second Saturday in December.

The game has been played most often (82 times!) in Philadelphia—neutral territory, a historic city, and about halfway between the academies.

Only six games have been played at the academies themselves. The first four games alternated between West Point and Annapolis. And then in 1942 and 1943, the games were played on campus to cut down on travel costs during wartime. Travel was so severely restricted that the Corps of Cadets was not allowed to attend the 1942 game at Annapolis, and half of the Brigade of Midshipmen were ordered to sit on the Army side of the field and cheer for West Point. Navy won the game 14–0.

In 1905, Woodrow Wilson, then the president of Princeton University, successfully lobbied for the game to be played in Princeton, New Jersey.

Eleven games have been played in New York City—at the Polo Grounds and Yankee Stadium.

Four games have been played in Baltimore.

In 1926, the game moved to Chicago for the dedication of Soldier Field.

Four games have been played at Giants Stadium, in East Rutherford, New Jersey.

In 1983, the city of Pasadena, California, paid the travel expenses for both the teams *and* the students of both schools so it could host the Army-Navy game at the Rose Bowl Stadium. This is the only game in this epic rivalry to have been played west of the Mississippi River.

The 2010 game will be played in Philadelphia, and the 2011 game is slated to take place in Landover, Maryland, outside Washington, D.C.

Presidents at the Army-Navy Game

Theodore Roosevelt was the first president to attend the game, which he did in 1901. He began the tradition of changing sides at halftime. Roosevelt also attended in 1902, and in 1905 he is said to have walked the sidelines, cheering on the teams.

Woodrow Wilson attended the game in 1913 at New York's Polo Grounds.

Calvin Coolidge attended the game in 1922 as vice president and then in 1926 as president.

Harry Truman attended the "game of the century" in 1945. And he returned in 1946, 1948, and 1950.

Dwight D. Eisenhower was the only future president ever to participate in the rivalry, starting at halfback and line-backer for Army in their 1912 loss. He attended the game once during his eight-year presidency.

Having served in the navy during World War II, President John F. Kennedy took great interest in the game, attending in 1961 and 1962. He started the tradition of performing the pregame coin toss. Kennedy took particular interest in the 1963 team, led by quarterback Roger Staubach, and he even visited Navy's preseason training camp to offer support. That year, Staubach won the Heisman Trophy and the team went 8–1 and was number two in the nation. Then eight days before the Army-Navy game was scheduled, President Kennedy was assassinated, and the game was canceled. But First Lady Jackie Kennedy felt that playing the game would be a fitting tribute, so the game was rescheduled at Municipal Stadium in Philadelphia a week later. The stadium was renamed John F. Kennedy Stadium in 1964.

After Kennedy's death, security concerns prevented many of his successors from attending the game. Between 1963 and 1995, only Gerald Ford attended—in 1974 to celebrate the 75th playing of the Army-Navy game.

Bill Clinton went to the game in a driving rainstorm in 1996—the first president to attend in twenty-two years.

George W. Bush attended the game three times (in 2001, 2004, and 2008), performing the coin toss and crossing midfield at halftime. In 2004, he also began a tradition of visiting the teams in their locker rooms before the game.

The only nonpresident ever granted access to both the Army and Navy locker rooms before, during, and after an Army-Navy game: John Feinstein, in 1995, while he was researching *A Civil War*.

Fun Facts and Firsts

In the 1893 game, Navy midshipman Joseph Mason Reeves wore what many regard as the first football helmet. He had been told that another kick to the head could result in "instant insanity" or even death, so he had a shoemaker fashion a helmet of leather. The NCAA did not require players to wear helmets until 1939.

"Anchors Aweigh," the Navy fight song, made its debut in the 1906 Army-Navy game. Navy won for the first time in five years.

The 1915 game at the Polo Grounds in New York was the first game in which players wore numbers on their uniforms.

Instant replay was used for the first time on any telecast during the Army-Navy game, in 1963.

In 1991 and again in 2000, Navy had only one win in the season—against Army.

Superlative Stats

Most touchdown passes in an Army-Navy game: 3, by George Welsh, Navy, in 1954.

Most receptions: 10, by Mike Clark, Navy, 1967.

Most receiving yards in one game: 128 yards, by Ryan Read, Navy, 1998.

Most interceptions: 4, by Mark Schickner, Navy, 1970.

Highest punting average: 57.6 yards per punt, by Joe Sartiano, Army, 1981.

Longest punt: 79 yards, by Joe Sartiano, Army, 1981.

Longest punt return: 81 yards, by Paul Johnson, Army, 1933.

Most kicking points: 15, by Steve Fehr, Navy, 1980.

Longest kickoff return (tie): 98 yards, by Charles Daly, Army, 1981, and by Reggie Campbell, Navy, 2007.

Longest rush from scrimmage: 92 yards, by Rip Rowan, Army, 1947.

Longest pass: 69 yards, by Brian Broadwater to Ryan Read, Navy, 1998.

Longest field goal: 52 yards, by Kurt Heiss, Army, 1994 (to win the game).

Longest interception return: 101 yards, by John Raster, Navy, 1951.

Sources for Further Reading

armynavygame.com/the-rivalry/timeline

phillylovesarmynavy.com/RIVALRY-HISTORY

goarmysports.com

navysports.com

gvsu.edu/hauenstein (Hauenstein Center for Presidential Studies)

A Civil War: Army vs. Navy—A Year Inside Football's Purest Rivalry
    by John Feinstein